"What's this, what's this?" the old voice sang. "Has our other pathway awoken?"

When Annie saw the head rise, she tried to scream and couldn't.

Staring at her, less than a touch away, was a gruesome half face. Strips of linen clung to the sunken cheeks where bone glistened, and the front teeth, yellow and black, were as large and bucked as a beaver's. Then Annie saw the eyes for the first time, eyes set in the bony sockets of the mummy.

Annie tried to scream again, but the mummy placed a musty hand over her mouth. It was freckled. When the mummy took the hand away, Annie saw the opal friendship ring on the mummy's finger.

Annie felt queasy. Suddenly she fell to the floor. Before she passed out, she felt hundreds of tiny legs tickling her body, and then some on her face. She thought she saw rats running across her nose. Then, mercifully, she saw nothing. . . .

ARE YOU AFRAID OF THE DARK?™ novels

Available from MINSTREL Books

NICKELODEON®

Are You Afraid of the Dark?®

THE TALE OF THE EGYPTIAN MUMMIES

MARK MITCHELL

A MINSTREL® BOOK

Published by POCKET BOOKS
New York   London   Toronto   Sydney   Tokyo   Singapore

A MINSTREL PAPERBACK *Original*

 A Minstrel Book published by
POCKET BOOKS, a division of Simon & Schuster Inc.
1230 Avenue of the Americas, New York, NY 10020

ISBN: 0-671-02112-5

First Minstrel Books printing July 1998

10 9 8 7 6 5 4 3 2 1

Cover art by Broeck Steadman

Printed in the U.S.A.

To Marie, Allie, Claire, Ted, and my pal Mundy,
of course.

THE TALE OF THE
EGYPTIAN MUMMIES

Prologue: The Midnight Society

Are you afraid of the dark? Well, come closer to the campfire and stare at it until you forget we're out in the middle of the woods. Besides, I like to see the faces of my fellow members of the Midnight Society when I have an especially scary story to tell. Hey, Frank, throw another log on the fire. We're going to need maybe two or three more of the big seasoned logs before I finish tonight.

My name is Samantha, and I'm sitting in this chair made out of big rocks. It protects me, and since it's solid stone, I don't have to keep looking behind me, wondering if something is sneaking up on me. Rock solid. Like a best friend, it protects my back.

Or would it? Is your best friend rock solid? Do you really know how to be someone's best friend? When things get tough, can you count on your friend's loyalty? Can your friend count on you? What if an ancient horror

1

from five thousand years ago—no, two ancient horrors— tried to come between you and your friend? Would you do the right thing?

I don't know what you would do, and you don't have to tell me. But I do know about two girls, best of friends from an early age, who confronted that question. You see, Annie Carr's best friend, Laura, moved away, which would cause a strain in any friendship. . . .

Well, I'm getting ahead of myself, so maybe I'd just better start from the beginning. Submitted for the approval of the Midnight Society, I call this story . . .

The Tale of the Egyptian Mummies.

CHAPTER 1

Annie Carr turned around and looked out the rear window of the boxy silver bus. The highway cut a straight path through the cornfields. Her home was three hundred miles back that way. She had been on the bus half the day, and the closer she got to the Mississippi River, the more her stomach bothered her. She was nervous about seeing her best friend Laura.

Annie didn't bounce a lot on the seat as she did on the creaky yellow school bus at home. This seat was for grown-ups, and it had a lever on the side so you could adjust the seat back. And just as Annie pulled the lever up to lean back and stretch her tight muscles, the bus sped up again. Annie braced her hands on the armrests as the bus accelerated to fight gravity, but she was thrown down with the seat anyway. Annie shook her head, wondering who the bus driver was trying to pass this time.

She sat up and craned her head forward to look out the big square window. Yup. Another red sportscar, this one a Mustang. This bus driver thought the highway was a racetrack. But it was no skin off her nose. The faster he drove, the sooner Annie would see her best friend. And that was good because she hadn't seen Laura D'Orrico since January, six long months ago.

Annie put her nose to the window and gazed at the fields of knee-high green corn, which she didn't like to eat, as the bus belched and settled into the right-hand lane once again. The countryside flattened out more the closer she got to the Mississippi River and Midwest University. Annie lived in hill country back East, so the first far horizons had taken her breath away before the flatness became boring. But now they headed up a little rise.

Suddenly she saw the big muddy river as they crested the top. The river was wide and brown and looked as if it had eaten too much recently. Laura had told her the river had flooded because of heavy rains up North, and the moving waters looked like an amoeba sending out fat, slimy arms to wrap around houses and trees.

Annie got the chills thinking about how great it would be to see Laura. Annie had called Laura yesterday to confirm her arrival time, and as usual the conversation had lasted half an hour. They talked about silly old things, and it was as if Laura had moved away yesterday instead of six months ago, Laura teasing her like always . . .

"So, Annie, maybe you better not come," Laura said, abruptly changing the subject.

4

"Yeah, right, Laura, after six months of planning and waiting, you want to cancel?" Annie asked.

Laura guffawed into the phone, and Annie held it away from her ear. Laura had the loudest laugh Annie had ever heard. It was a laugh that made people jump.

"Well, Annie, I've never forgiven you for giving me that noogie in first grade. It still hurts when I think about it."

Annie smiled. "That's because you're stubborn. No one stole your lunch five years ago. Remember, you found it in your backpack, not mine. I had to calm you down with the noogie."

Laura guffawed again. "It's funny how people get to know each other, isn't it, Annie? I mean, who would have thought we could become best friends after starting out angry at each other?"

"Well, look at Robin Hood and Little John. And how about—"

"Aw, you and your heroes, Annie."

"There's nothing wrong with helping underdogs, Laura."

"Well, okay, Ms. Underdog helper, how come you never write or e-mail me first? How come I have to keep in touch?"

"I always write back to you. Unless I have nothing to say."

"Well, why don't you treat me like an underdog sometime and write or call me first?"

"I do."

"Tell me the last time you called me first."

"Today. To tell you the time my bus arrives tomorrow. One P.M."

Laura shot back, *"I asked you that in an e-mail last night. Try again."*

Whew, *Annie thought*, what's with Laura? She sounded almost serious about this.

"Uh, Valentine's Day?"

"That was four months ago, Annie."

"Is something bothering you, Laura?"

Laura sighed. "No, other things are on my mind, I guess."

"Like what?"

"Just other things."

"Are you starting to keep secrets from me, Laura?"

"Why would I do that?" Laura snapped, and before Annie could react, Laura laughed a deep, hard laugh. Laura, the practical joker.

"No secrets. Except . . . oh, Annie, I forgot to tell you. Chloe had her kittens! And since Chloe seems to like you so much, maybe you can have one of the litter. Or take the whole bunch," Laura said, and she sneezed. *"Chloe still doesn't let anyone touch her except for you and my dad. And me sometimes, but she's been picky about me lately. At least she helps with the rats. They've been crawling all over campus since the Mississippi flooded."*

"Rats? Do you mean mice?"

"No. Rats. Big ones. Chloe seems jumpy all the time."

"Don't laugh so hard around her."

"Chloe can take it. Anyway, we'll have a lot of fun, Annie. My dad will be holed up studying his mummies, so we'll be on our own a lot. My dad spends more time with them than with me, and I'm lonely. I can't wait to see you."

"Really, Laura? I miss seeing you every day. Remem-

6

ber those bike rides, and spending every day together in the summer? I miss that."

"And talking about the goofy things fifth-grade boys do? They're the same out here." The laugh erupted, and this time it sounded like a honk.

"That laugh grew on me," Annie said.

"Well, you make me laugh, Annie, even when you don't know it."

"Is that an insult?" Annie asked, but she was smiling.

"Ah, be quiet. It's a compliment. See you tomorrow."

"It's going to be great to see you again, Laura."

"Just you remember that," Laura said, and then she hung up before Annie could ask what she meant by that.

Annie pulled her head away from the window of the bus, not realizing she had been leaning against the glass. She wiped the window where her breath had made a misty fog.

This trip was important. It was Annie's chance to get the friendship back on track, in person, to live the way she had done for the past five years. Laura and Annie had lived on the same block. Annie wished for the hundredth time that she could see her best friend every day because she didn't want their friendship to fade away. But maybe their friendship was doomed. Out of sight, out of mind, that sort of thing.

A sign caught Annie's eye, and she shook herself out of her thoughts. "Welcome to Midwest University, Home of the Wildcats."

Annie grew excited as she looked at all the ivy covering the brick walls. Soon she'd see her best friend.

And then Annie almost got sick, but not from the

anticipation of seeing Laura or from the acrid scent of the bus.

A herd of big grayish brown rats ran and tumbled over one another as they sprinted around the corner of the nearest building. There were hundreds of rats, and the few students on campus for summer session scattered as the herd spread out on open ground.

In a flash Annie saw what caused the rat stampede. A dozen cats came flying into view, their bodies leaning into the curve to race around the building corner at high speed. They were chasing the rats. One cat caught a rat in its mouth and shook it like a rag doll before tossing it aside. The rat bounced twice and jumped up, looking directly at Annie. It had blood-red eyes which penetrated like laser beams. The heads of the other rats seemed to turn in one sea of motion to stare at her. The fiery redness beaming from the little mammalian skulls looked spooky.

Annie tore her gaze away when the rats resumed running. The cats followed. One of them looked *exactly* like Chloe. Annie was sure it was Laura's cat. But Chloe had just had kittens. *This* can't *be Chloe! Can it?* What was going on?

The bus braked with a long hiss and came to a complete stop as Annie's head did a chicken peck. Another hiss and the bus door opened.

Annie skipped down the steps of the bus, still queasy about the rats. Young people slapped confident sneakers and clogs on the cold cement floor as they hurried in all directions through the dark bus station. Annie squinted, her eyes adjusting to the whirling dust and the brown shadows bouncing off the paneled walls. Suddenly, above the rumble of the buses and the shouts of college kids greeting friends, Annie heard . . . the laugh.

"Laura!" Annie yelled, whirling to spot her friend. Annie ran toward the laugh, but then hesitated and stopped in front of a stranger who looked a little like Laura.

"Hi, Annie," the stranger said.

Annie shook her head and blinked her eyes. The stranger couldn't be Laura. The girl standing in front of Annie had dark, almost black hair, and only one of her arms had freckles. The other arm was coppery brown. And the hand attached to the coppery arm had no rings. Laura always wore the opal friendship ring Annie had given her. Nope, this wasn't Laura, her pretty brunette friend with the remarkable red streaks in her hair.

And how come one arm was freckled and one was tanned? Weird. Was this girl Laura's cousin? The girl's eyes were darker brown than Laura's, too. Almost as black as the pupils. Who was she?

"Annie," the girl said in a deep voice. "It's me."

"Who is me?" Annie asked very politely as she stood at attention, acting formal. But then she giggled. Things were strange.

The stranger slapped her thigh and erupted into a guffaw that drew startled looks from people crisscrossing through the bus station. The laugh was Laura's. Unmistakably the foghorn bark of Laura D'Orrico. Suddenly Annie felt completely unsure of herself.

"Oh, Annie, you'll never change. You'll always make me laugh," said Laura—the new, grown-up Laura. She stepped forward and hugged Annie, squeezing her tight.

9

Annie melted a bit, feeling good. She knew this hug. It was the hug Laura had given her in January, when they said good-bye. Annie suddenly felt foolish she had failed to recognize Laura. Laura had just grown up a bit, right? Annie opened her eyes and saw that up close Laura's hair really was darker. Annie remembered the apple shampoo Laura used, but when she let her nose take in the scent of Laura's hair, Annie received a big shock. Instead of the scent of fresh apples, all Annie smelled was the musty scent of wet newspapers that had dried. Annie gagged. Why did her friend smell musty?

Laura grabbed Annie by both arms and smiled at her. "Oh, Annie, I'm so glad you're here. I've really missed you. You look exactly the same."

Annie smiled back, but her smile was crooked. This was all too weird.

"Annie, what's wrong?"

Annie stared at Laura and said, "You've changed . . . so much."

Laura guffawed again, but this time it trailed off instead of ending in a sharp bark.

"Is that good or bad?" Laura asked. She wore a loose-fitting dress. Laura had seven pairs of jeans, some white, some blue, one for every day of the week. Laura had owned a single dress when Annie knew her, and it wasn't this flowing thing.

Annie shrugged. "Well, you seem so grown up. I haven't seen you in six months, but . . . your hair . . . and your arm. What happened to your arm?"

Laura's eyes flashed coldly, scaring Annie, and then the sparkle returned.

10

"I have a little skin problem," Laura said, a bit sad, and Annie felt stupid for asking about it in the bus station. *Annie,* she scolded herself, *why are you acting so shocked? Laura is your best friend. Calm down.*

Laura sounded like her old self, except for the deeper voice, but she looked so different. Why? Was this one of her practical jokes?

"Hey, come on, Annie. My dad wants us to stop by the lab to make sure you got here okay. He promised to show us those girl mummies the museum is testing for the Egyptian government. Really interesting mummies. They found them way out in the Sahara, hundreds of miles from the Nile River, hundreds of miles from everything. They were in a cave near an oasis that was guarded by hundreds of cats—yuck—and there were hieroglyphics with horrible curses all over the walls. Is that cool or what? I can't wait to show them to you."

Laura picked up Annie's small bag and started walking.

Annie stood there a moment, her mouth in an oval. She controlled her shock and followed Laura, her mind racing.

Laura interested in mummies? Laura hated mummies.

Laura saying "yuck" about cats? Laura loved cats, especially Chloe.

Laura with darker hair and one coppery arm and dark brown eyes?

When she added it all up, Annie was sure of one thing. It didn't add up to Laura. And now Annie was really scared. She wasn't sure why, but she was really scared. Three-hundred-miles-from-home scared.

11

CHAPTER 2

Annie followed Laura on the curved path. Suddenly Laura stopped and put down Annie's bag. She hugged Annie again and said, "It's like I saw you yesterday. You don't know how much I've looked forward to your visiting me. We're going to have so much fun!"

Annie looked at Laura and she could feel a tear forming in the corner of her eye. She quickly wiped it, not wanting Laura to see her cry. "I hope so, Laura. I mean I really missed you, too. In fact, I was a little worried about us. I got the impression you didn't want me to visit. We used to e-mail each other every day, and then it slowed down, and then you kept putting off the visit, and there's nobody back home who could take your place, and I figured that you found another—"

"Whoa, girl, time out," Laura said, and she made the letter *T* with her hands.

12

Annie raised her eyebrows.

"Look, Annie, you're my best friend, and you always will be. In fact, it was *me* who asked *you* to visit. Remember yesterday's phone conversation? *I* stay in touch."

"Oh, Laura, I know. I want to be best friends . . . forever."

Laura's eyes flashed again as they had in the bus station. They seemed a little cruel for a second, and then they regained their brightness.

"Hey, Annie," she chided, smiling. "Nice wish. Sounds like you mean it."

"That's what I want," Annie said, and got a chill when Laura's right eyebrow hiked up a bit.

Everything will be fine, Annie thought. Annie cocked her head and said, "You know, Laura, I couldn't wait to get here. But I've got to tell you, six months must be a long time. You look so grown-up. Like a lady or something."

Laura barked out a long, hard laugh, and Annie jumped. She was getting used to the laugh again, and it was the laugh that reminded her that Laura was her best friend, even if she looked a little different. So what if she looked a little older. People change. Laura certainly looked . . . older.

Annie smiled her crooked smile and sighed. She said, "Laura, are you wearing a . . . you know . . . under that dress?"

Laura said, "Ha! You mean a bikini top?"

"Well, sort of . . ."

"You bet I am. It's summer, and that's what the college girls wear so that they can sun themselves by the Ole Miss between classes."

"Wow," Annie said.

"Here, take a look," Laura said, and she lifted her dress up over her head to reveal that she wore cutoff jeans and a bikini top.

Annie couldn't believe it. Not the fact that Laura had sacrificed a pair of jeans with her scissors. She always did that in the summer. It was her left leg. It was brown, and it didn't have freckles. Just like her coppery brown arm. That skin problem was widespread.

They walked a bit more, Annie trying to process everything about her arrival, taking in the sights of the college, worried about her best friend, but maybe she didn't have to be worried. Laura had changed, but she didn't want a new best friend. That was good.

"Here's the lab building," Laura said, and she pushed the door in.

In a minute they were outside a door with a keypad lock.

Laura entered a security code, and the door buzzed open.

"Valuable mummies with valuable jewelry," Laura explained. "I have the code because I have to come drag my dad home every once in a while. He gets so wrapped up in his work."

"Well, that's what mummies will do to you," Annie replied innocently, and then she heard the guffaw. Annie slapped her forehead.

"Annie Carr!" The voice of Dr. D'Orrico boomed across the large room, and the sound snapped Annie

14

away from the strong odor of wet newspapers that had dried. The lab smelled just like Laura's hair.

Dr. D'Orrico came bounding over and shook Annie's hand. Dr. D'Orrico was a proper man, and he always treated Annie like an adult. Except for Laura, he didn't hug anybody. He just gave people that businesslike handshake.

"My goodness, Annie, you haven't changed a bit."

"Hi, Dr. D'Orrico. That's what Laura said. It's good to see you. Thanks for letting me visit."

"Oh, it's our pleasure. Laura has been bugging me to let you come for months. Now I'll be able to get some real work done without getting pestered three times a day."

Laura frowned. "Don't exaggerate, Daddy. You work too hard all the time. I never see you."

Dr. D'Orrico slumped against the lab counter and rubbed at the dark circles under his eyes. Then he took a deep breath and said, in a low, low voice, "Honey, I know I haven't been around. It's just that I have to return the new mummies to Egypt in a week, and I have hundreds more tests to do. This is the most important work I've ever done. I thought you understood."

Laura crossed her arms, but she softened her frown right before she spoke. "I understand, Daddy, but you get home at nine every night and then you eat a bowl of soup and go right to bed. I can't even wake you for phone calls because you're so sound asleep. When you finish with these mummies, I bet someone will send you one from Peru or Russia, and it will be the same thing all over."

15

Dr. D'Orrico approached Laura with his arms out-stretched, and Annie knew he was going to hug her. It eased her discomfort at watching Laura and her dad fight over his work. Annie knew Laura was upset at moving here, but she had never heard Laura jump down her dad's throat.

Laura suddenly turned away from her father, avoiding the hug, and Annie cringed. Notwithstanding the fight that had made Laura her best friend, Annie had always been a peacemaker, so she jumped in to fix things, or at least blunt the argument.

"Hey, Dr. D'Orrico, tell me about the mummies." Annie walked over to the glass chambers that kept the mummies as dry as if they were still in the Sahara. She looked in the glass and gasped. The mummies were small and shriveled, their necks thin as shovel handles, the skin black and tight over the bones, like some strange plastic wrap. They were skeletal, with the long yellow teeth pro-truding out from thin black lips. Wisps of long black hair sprouted from the round skulls in a few spots, and Annie thought they were the ugliest-looking things she had ever seen. It almost made her sick to her stomach.

"Beautiful, aren't they?" Dr. D'Orrico asked as he slid next to Annie. Annie's eyebrows shot up in surprise, and Laura laughed, but it wasn't *the* laugh. This was muted, almost sarcastic.

"These bodies were mummified almost five thousand years ago, Annie. Right at the time Pharaoh Cheops was building that huge pyramid at Giza. In fact, the hiero-glyphs on the tomb walls of these mummies referred to

16

Cheops and the trouble these two supposedly gave him as he was trying to get the pyramid built.''

"What?" Annie asked. "These two sorry-looking things gave a pharaoh trouble? I thought pharaohs were kings."

"Oh, yes, and more. You see, these mummies, if we are to believe the hieroglyphs, were dangerous witches in ancient Egypt. They were executed, mummified, and banished to a tomb far out in the Sahara, where nobody should have found them. And they wouldn't have been found if not for some sharp-eyed oil explorers."

"How did the oil explorers find them?"

Laura spoke from the corner. "The cats. Yuck."

Annie frowned. There it was again. Laura was dissing cats, completely unlike her. Chloe was so important to Laura. Right?

Dr. D'Orrico laughed. "Don't mind Laura. After Chloe had her litter, Laura got a little tired with all the cats around, and she blames the litter for her skin rash. And Chloe stopped paying her any attention because of the kittens. They need her, Laura. Don't be mad at Chloe."

Laura shrugged.

Annie asked, "What about the cats?"

"Well," Dr. D'Orrico continued, "there were hundreds of cats living in the tomb, and they looked like no cats you see today. These cats were scrawnier, with big ears, the kind that you see depicted in ancient Egyptian wall paintings. At least that's what the oilmen said. We have a couple of pictures, but the cats fled into the desert after the oilmen took the mummies. Seems the oilmen weren't fond of the cats. The cats attacked them when they tried to take the mummies, almost as if they were guarding the tomb. And there may be some credence to that, if you believe the hieroglyphs."

"The 'Rat Witches,'" Laura said sarcastically, and then she looked as if she wanted to cry. "I bet you those witches were terrible." Laura seemed to suffer a spasm, and then her new mature smile returned, and she said, "Terrible to cross. And very powerful."

"What?" Annie asked.

"Laura's right," Dr. D'Orrico said. "They were identified only as the Rat Witches on the wall paintings. Here's the story. Most people have always thought that the pyramids were built by slave labor. But now we are looking at a new theory. In order to get the necessary manpower to build these huge things, some of us think the Pharaoh accepted volunteer workers in the off-planting season to help build the pyramids. The Nile flooded annually. Before it receded and farmers could plant seeds for the next season's crop, the farmers would work on the pyramids. With the Nile at flood stage, they could float big stones right up to Giza. But it seems our Rat Witches here got mad at the Pharaoh for not establishing a Rat temple, and they visited a plague of rats on the people just as they were to go and help build the pyramids. The people spent all their time trying to eradicate the rats, and the Pharaoh Cheops was understandably upset. They got rid of the rats, and the Rat Witches were captured trying to flee to Luxor. They were executed and sent out into the desert. And since they were entombed outside Egypt, they couldn't go to the Next World."

"The Next World?" Annie asked.

"Sort of an ancient Egyptian heaven. That's why they mummified dead people and put them in tombs with riches and food and the things that the Egyptians would want to bring with them to the Next World. But these witches were entombed outside Egypt. And if you died or were buried outside Egypt, the Egyptians believed you could not get to the Next World. Sending them to the Sahara was probably just insurance. They most likely wouldn't have made it to the Next World anyway, based on the Egyptian Book of the Dead."

"I've heard of that," Annie said. "Isn't that the book that gave directions on how to get to . . . what do you call it? The Next World?"

"That's right, Annie. In order to get to the Next World, you had to live a good life on earth. When an Egyptian died, he believed he had to pass a series of tests to get to the Next World. The Book of the Dead had spells and directions. There were a number of tests."

"Tests?"

"First, you had to get across the River of Death. Then there were twelve massive gates guarded by giant snakes that you had to get past. Then, if you could get across the Lake of Fire, you had to go in front of the Forty-two Assessors, who reviewed all your sins. If you could explain your way out of them, you had to have your heart weighed against the Feather of Truth. If you had a lot of sins which made your heart heavy, you'd tip the scales. No Next World for heavy hearts. But if you'd been good, your heart would balance with the feather, and then you'd get to the Next World."

19

"Sounds complicated."

"Far too complicated for these two. Their hearts must have been heavy. They'd need new, light ones to get there. But it's a fascinating story. I'm still doing DNA tests and analyzing tissue to see how they died. Maybe they were poisoned, or maybe they were executed with the bite of an asp like Cleopatra was. Did you know that? But she wasn't executed, she—"

"Dad, we've got to get going," Laura said. "Do you have the laundry?"

"Oh, sure, Laura. In the bag over there."

Laura looked at Annie and said, "Our basement got flooded and ruined the washing machine, so we're using the industrial-strength machines next door at the gym. Wanna help?"

"Sure," Annie said. "Thanks for the info on the mummies, Dr. D'Orrico. I had no idea there was so much to all that stuff."

"My pleasure, Annie. I'm glad you're here. Laura, I'll try to make it back early tonight. And be careful. They still haven't found those two college kids. If I'm late, why don't you two order a pizza or something."

Laura shook her head and walked out without replying.

Dr. D'Orrico watched her go and said to Annie, "Growing up isn't easy. Thanks for coming, Annie. To tell you the truth, I'm hoping you can help get Laura back to normal. She's been angry a lot lately. I don't really blame her, but she was always happy when you were around, even when I worked late. I want my little girl back."

20

Annie shrugged and said, "I'll do what I can. She's my best friend, and I don't . . . want to lose my best friend." Why had she said that? And what could she do about it? Laura either liked her or she didn't. Annie was embarrassed a second, and then she said, "I'll see you later, Dr. D'Orrico." She ran to catch up with Laura before she lost sight of her.

Inside the gym Annie found Laura next to a huge front-loading washing machine, where Laura was throwing in a load of white clothes.

"Gee, Laura, what was that all about?" Annie asked. "You sure were hard on him."

"Oh, Annie, grow up. I'm just mad, that's all."

Laura threw detergent into the machine and started it. "Oh, no, I left money in my white pants." Laura turned off the machine and stuck in her arm, the freckled one. She pulled out the white jeans and stuck her other hand into the pocket, and then she gasped and pulled her hand out, the coppery brown one. Laura screamed, and Annie looked to see what was wrong. Her hand, the one with the skin problem, was actually smoking, as if it were burning.

"Laura, are you okay?" Annie asked, confused and upset about her friend. She didn't know what to make of the smoking hand. "What's wrong, Laura?"

"Oh, it's my skin problem. The rash is really sensitive to water. I take sponge baths now."

"Oh," Annie said. Well, maybe that explained the musty smell. Laura hadn't been taking any showers. But that smoking hand was really weird.

"Laura, did your hand actually burn? It looked like smoke for a minute."

Laura cackled like her old self and said, "That's a good one. I get my arm wet, and you think it's burning. You kill me, Annie."

CHAPTER
3

The pizza man was late.

"It's a quarter after eight," Laura said, shaking her head. "Maybe he's the next person to go missing. The rumors are flying all over about those missing college girls."

Annie was a little unnerved about the missing-person talk. Things like that didn't happen at home, or at least she wasn't aware of it. "He's not *that* late," Annie said. "Does anyone have a clue as to why those girls disappeared?"

"No," Laura said, but she wouldn't look at Annie. Annie got a strange feeling—these sensations were becoming standard ever since she arrived here—that Laura somehow knew more than just "no." Maybe she didn't want to upset Annie.

Annie stuck her head back in the afternoon newspaper. The article about the rat infestation on campus fascinated her. The pest-control person quoted in the paper said he had never seen anything like it in his forty-three years of living on the Mississippi. They were laying poisoned rat food all over campus, and he warned people to keep a close eye on their pets so they wouldn't eat the poisoned food, or the poisoned rats for that matter. He warned people to keep their cats and dogs inside. Annie started, wondering where Chloe was. And then she remembered the kittens.

"Where are Chloe and the kittens?" she asked. "Can I see them?"

Laura closed her eyes and then slowly opened them. "I had to put them in the basement. I'm sure that I'm becoming allergic to cat hair. It aggravates my skin condition." Laura peered around, as if she was looking for someone. She seemed to be in pain, and said, "I really like Chloe, Annie." Then she shrugged, her eyes rolling up into her head. When she opened her eyelids, she added a few testy words. "I like Chloe to stay in the basement, so if you look for the kittens, keep Chloe down there."

Annie was confused. Laura was acting hot and cold again, just as she had at her dad's laboratory.

Annie almost started to say something about how lackadaisical Laura had become, especially about her favorite pet Chloe, but she bit her tongue. She'd confront Laura later, after they had gotten used to being together again. Annie needed to take it all in rather than accuse her best friend about changes. And after all, hadn't

Laura said today that she still wanted to be best friends forever?

Annie followed Laura to the basement door. Laura opened it and switched on the light, and Annie suddenly heard a soft hissing. Laura jumped back. "You little brat," she spat at the stairs. Then she looked sheepishly at Annie and said, "I didn't mean that . . . really, I . . ."

"It's okay," Annie replied. But she knew it wasn't.

Annie looked at the stairs and saw a tiny gray kitten, its back arched, the hair along its spine raised and separated, a scowl on its face. The kitten hissed at Laura, who hissed back, a mean scowl on her face.

Laura stepped away. "Make sure you keep the door closed."

Annie picked up the kitten, who relaxed immediately, retracting its tiny claws as she cuddled the little furball in her palms. She held the kitty to her face, and a rough little tongue lapped at her ear, making Annie giggle. She walked downstairs and saw Chloe and her brood in a pillowed basket. Chloe reclined, unmoving, and a half dozen kittens in shades of gray and tan rolled over her and one another. Chloe watched Annie approach, and Annie put the little gray down. Instead of running to its mother, the gray pawed at the laces on Annie's sneaker.

"Oh, you poor little things, confined to the basement. As soon as Laura's skin gets better, I'm sure she'll love you all just as much as I do, and I just met you guys." Annie peered up the stairs. "At least, I hope she'll love you."

Chloe suddenly turned her head to look in a dark corner, and then jumped up, her head unmoving, staring at something in the corner. The basement smelled dank from being flooded. Annie's eyes followed Chloe's to a shadowy angle formed where the floor joined the cement basement wall.

Annie jumped. Two sets of red eyes were beaming out of the corner. Chloe ran to the corner, and the red eyes disappeared, and then Chloe slowed, sniffed the area, and returned to her kittens. Could the red eyes have been rats? Ugh!

The doorbell rang and Annie heard Laura clomping on the floor above to answer the door. Annie was hungry despite thinking about the rats.

"Hey, kitties, it's time for my dinner, but I promise to visit you real soon. You're all adorable. Good job, Chloe."

Annie bounded up the stairs, the little gray pouncing at her ankles the whole way. Annie had to keep the kitten from following her, gently pushing it back as she closed the basement door.

"The kittens are gorgeous!" Annie said as she grabbed a slice of pepperoni, and Laura coughed and yelled, "Annie, wash your hands!"

They ate the pizza with hardly a word between them, the slurping of soda and the smacking of lips the bulk of the conversation.

"You want that last piece, Laura?" Annie asked.

"No, go ahead. I'm real tired. I need to go to bed. You can sleep in the top bunk. It has fresh sheets."

"Okay, Laura. Can't wait to get up and do some things with you tomorrow."

Laura stopped, staring at Annie. She looked as if she

wanted to cry, but she swallowed, managed a smile, and said, "Look, Annie, this has been a pretty rough day, and I know I'm pretty much to blame. It's just that . . . my skin really bothers me, my dad's been ignoring me, and I've been having terrible nightmares. I feel bad that you think I changed so much, but I promise you we'll have a great time together while you're here. I really want to be best friends forever. But if I don't feel better, maybe you should go home. . . ."

Annie stopped in mid-bite—*go home?* Again? A Laura practical joke? Annie's discomfort must have been plastered on her face, because Laura went to Annie's side. She hugged Annie, who had a tough time putting her arms around Laura since she was holding the last slice of pepperoni pizza in her hand, but she managed to return Laura's hug without spilling pepperoni on her friend. Laura smiled and went to her room.

Annie watched her go, and a tear fell from her eye, feelings of relief competing with her sense of disappointment about how Laura had changed. *Maybe that's what growing up is about,* she thought. *Things don't stay the same forever.* But if she and Laura could work through this, maybe they'd become even better friends. Just like after the fight that had launched their friendship.

But what had Laura meant about going home? Annie had just arrived.

Dr. D'Orrico came home while Annie was picking up in the kitchen. He seemed really tired, said good night, and went to bed. Annie watched a little television, and soon she could hear Dr. D'Orrico snoring down the hall. The show was boring, so Annie stared out the picture window into the black night, thinking about Laura, thinking about how her own life wasn't as rich without Laura around, feeling a little homesick because everything was so strange here. Rats, mummies, Laura hating cats . . .

Suddenly Annie jumped. Something was framed in the picture window.

She was certain there was a person staring in at her. There were no lights outside, and the shadow of the person moved away without Annie getting a good glimpse.

Annie was paralyzed. She forced herself to stand up, and then she turned out the lights. With her heart pounding, she moved toward and tried the front door. She was relieved to find that it was locked. She waited there a minute or two but heard nothing. Maybe she'd imagined it. But, no, somebody had been out there. She peeked out the window. Nothing. The person had left. She decided not to wake Dr. D'Orrico. She'd tell him about the prowler tomorrow.

She tiptoed into Laura's room and hurriedly put on her pajamas, then climbed to the top bunk and pulled the covers all the way over her face. When she thought about being in the top bunk, she worried that she would fall out, so she made sure the covers were tucked tight under the mattress to keep her wrapped like a cocoon.

It took her awhile, but she finally felt she had slipped into sleep. And then the nutty dream came.

It was weird. Annie saw herself in Laura's room under the blankets, all the way under the blankets, but she could still see the room, or at least a portion of it. At the end of the bunk bed a row of red eyes stared at her, more than ten sets of eyes. She was glad it was a dream, but she felt scared just the same, and the more the eyes stared, the more afraid she became. She had to go to the bathroom, but she wouldn't move. It was a dream after all, right?

Then she thought she saw the bedroom door open, but only for a second, and only just a crack.

Her eyes were accustomed to the dark in her dream—sort of—and she thought she saw a head bobbing up and down, coming toward the bunk beds. And then the musty scent of wet newspapers that had dried invaded her nose, and she could see the top of the bobbing head. It was wrapped in old linen, and tufts of feathery hair sprang out at odd angles from the linen. Just like those mummies in Dr. D'Orrico's lab!

It's just a dream, Annie told herself. *You've had nightmares like this before, Annie. Just keep your head and everything will be fine.*

But then a voice broke the silence. Annie opened her eyes. The tiny red pinpoints of light arrayed along the bottom of her bed had grown from ten to a hundred, and Annie felt a weight pressing on her feet. *It's just a dream. It's just a dream.*

The voice wafted up from below, from Laura's bed, and it cackled, hoarse, harsh, in a language Annie couldn't understand, speaking syllables in rhythm, the cadence up and down, singsongy.

And then the voice spoke English.

"That is good, my dear, drink up, drink up, drink up. We shall soon be one and you shall be none, and then the Next World will be ours, for your heart and that of your friend are as light as feathers. Drink up, drink up, drink up. Tonight we take the kittens. Such nice tails," the voice sang, lyrical yet harsh.

Annie blinked, and now she realized she was wide awake. It was not a dream. Her heart pumped wildly, and she could feel yellow adrenaline—she didn't know why she thought the adrenaline was yellow—rushing through her veins, and she sat straight up with a moan.

"What's this, what's this?" the old voice sang. "Has our other pathway awoken?"

Annie saw the head rise, the chin level with the mattress, and then Annie tried to scream but couldn't.

Staring at her, less than a touch away, was a gruesome half face, as dark as the night in the room, but fully visible. Strips of linen clung to the sunken cheeks where bone glistened, and the front teeth, yellow and black, pointed at her because they were as large and bucked as a beaver's. Then Annie saw the eyes for the first time. The lids had been closed in the lab. She had seen the eyes thousands of times before. The eyes belonged to Laura D'Orrico. But they were set in the bony sockets of the mummy.

Annie tried to scream again, but the mummy placed a hand over her mouth. The hand smelled musty, but not as musty as the rest of the mummy. And it was freckled. And when the mummy took her hand away, Annie saw the opal friendship ring on the mummy's finger.

Annie screamed finally and jumped to the floor. She looked past the mummy to the bottom bunk, and strangely, there was Laura. She held a beaker containing a small amount of blue liquid. The same blue liquid covered Laura's lips. What was going on?

Annie felt queasy. Suddenly she fell to the floor. Before she passed out, she felt hundreds of tiny legs tickling her body, and then some on her face. She thought she saw rats running across her nose. Then, mercifully, she saw nothing.

CHAPTER
4

Annie felt her shoulder being rolled around and opened her eyes. Her nose was pressed against the floor, and the dust made her sneeze.

"Bless you," said Dr. D'Orrico. His hand was on Annie's shoulder. He had woken her. Annie saw bright sunshine outside when she pushed herself to a sitting position. She looked up and saw the covers from the top bunk streaming down.

"Are you okay, Annie?" Laura asked. She was rubbing her eyes.

"What am I doing on the floor?" Annie asked, bewildered, and not a little embarrassed.

Dr. D'Orrico smiled. "That's what we were going to ask you."

Annie stood and rubbed her head. There was a little knot just above her hairline that stung when she rubbed it. Rubbing her head caused her to recall the dream. She caught her scream and turned it into a harsh gasp.

"What?" Laura asked, her eyebrow arched, a smirk beginning to form around her mouth. A strange light flickered behind Laura's irises, and Annie watched with interest as first the eyes flashed hate, and then concern for Annie, and then selfish concern. Laura was struggling, but with what?

"Oh, I remember now," Annie said, shaking her head and looking away from Laura. "I had a horrible dream about—"

"About what?" Laura interrupted, and now there was a definite edge to the question.

"Cool it, Laura," Dr. D'Orrico demanded.

Laura looked at her dad and said, "Sorry."

"That's okay," Annie said. "You know, I'm having a hard time remembering. I fell out of bed . . . so it must have been a whopper."

Laura hopped out from under the covers. "Well, come on, Annie. We'll have to find that old guardrail for the bed so you don't break your neck. I'm glad you weren't hurt bad."

Dr. D'Orrico smiled at Annie and said, "How about a big breakfast for a couple of growing girls? Waffles?"

"Sure," Annie said, smiling. She loved breakfast.

"Don't get too excited, Annie," Laura said, giggling. "They're the toaster kind."

"But I'm a master at the toaster controls," Dr. D'Orrico said. "You'll see, Annie . . . Annie? What's the matter?"

Annie couldn't move. She stood straight at attention,

the hair lifting off the back of her neck, looking at Laura's mattress.

"Do you want *my* bed?" Laura asked.

Annie shivered and looked at Laura. "No . . . no, that's okay. I think I just remembered more of my dream. It's nothing, really."

But the blue stain the size of a half-dollar that formed an irregular circle on Laura's pillow was *something.* Something Annie didn't want to see. Laura had sipped blue liquid in Annie's dream. Or had Annie experienced a *real* nightmare? Annie started shaking, thinking about the little legs scurrying over her body last night. *It was just a dream. It was just a dream.* Annie tasted bile. She held a hand to her mouth and said, "You know, I'm really not hungry. Can I take a shower?"

Laura and her father shrugged. "Sure, honey," Dr. D'Orrico said. "Laura, show Annie where the towels are. Annie, are you feeling okay? Do you want to see a doctor? I'm concerned you might have a concussion."

Laura nodded in genuine concern. "Maybe she ought to go home, Dad."

Annie and Dr. D'Orrico frowned, and then Laura guffawed, throwing her head back. She said coldly, "Just kidding."

Dr. D'Orrico asked, "Do you want to go to the clinic?"

Annie was afraid, but not of the clinic. She screwed up a smile and said, "No, thanks. I'm fine, really. The water will wake me up."

After her shower Annie was able to eat some crispy

waffles. She and Laura then went to the basement to look for the bunk bed guardrail. Annie was surprised that Laura didn't hesitate when she opened the basement door. Completely unlike last night, when she had been worried about that poor little gray kitten. But no furballs greeted them, and Laura bounded down the stairs and over to a corner, whistling. Annie followed, looking for Chloe and her kittens. A musty smell much stronger than it had been last night assaulted her nostrils. And then Annie gasped. The wicker basket with the velvet pillow was empty. No Chloe. No kittens. No fur anywhere.

Laura was pulling on a wooden railing, scraping it on the floor. "Hey, Annie. You're strong. Give me a hand."

"Sure." Annie swept her eyes around the basement. No sign of Chloe and the kittens at all.

"Laura, where are the cats?" Annie asked as she grabbed one end of the railing.

"Huh? Oh, I don't know. Come on, let's bring this upstairs."

Laura started forward, but Annie held her ground, which caused Laura to halt. "Come on, Annie."

"Laura, where are the kittens? I know they bother your skin, but aren't you concerned? Have they been out of the house yet?"

"No. So maybe my dad let them out. Come on."

"Laura, I'm worried."

Laura stared at Annie, and she started to say something, but then she took a deep breath. Annie got the feeling Laura knew something more, just like when they had discussed the missing college girls. Laura shrugged and said, "Okay, we'll look for them. After we fix your bed so you don't fall out anymore. I don't want you falling on me." She let out a guffaw that made Annie jump and smile. But Annie's smile turned sour when she saw Laura's right arm—the one that still had the freckles. Or was supposed to have freckles. Now, both of Laura's arms were dark coppery brown.

Laura saw Annie's gaze and said sarcastically, "Yes, Annie dear, it's spreading."

But Annie wasn't as concerned about the arm as she was about the ring that now graced Laura's ring finger. It was the scarab beetle ring Annie had seen on the mummy only yesterday. She was certain of that.

"Laura, where'd you get the ring?"

Laura held her hand in front of her face. "Oh, this? My dad brought it home. It's a . . . replica . . . I think. Or maybe he's letting me wear it this week before the mummies have to be shipped back."

"Huh? Isn't it priceless?"

"No, there are replicas being sold on campus. I think it's like a peace offering. But don't embarrass him by mentioning it."

Annie almost shouted. Things were too weird. She was starting to wonder about her sanity. And she was questioning almost everything about her best friend. But the worst thing about it was she had every right to question Laura D'Orrico, and why Laura was struggling to be her friend one minute, and saying hateful things the next. She just didn't have the guts to do it right now. *Wait, Annie,* she thought. *Things will straighten themselves out soon. First things first. Chloe and the kittens.*

They started their search around the house, but there were no signs of Chloe or her brood.

Broadening their search to the next street, the girls were stopped by the captain and sergeant of the campus police, who were handing out photographs to passersby.

"Well, hello, Laura. Who's your friend?"

"Hi, Captain Cappello. This is Annie Carr from my old hometown. She's my best friend. And this is Sergeant Hannibal, Annie."

"How do, miss?" the officers asked, and they both politely doffed their blue caps.

"Laura, honey, have you or your friend seen these two girls in your wanderings?" Captain Cappello asked, and he handed the girls photographs. Annie looked at the two head shots. Both featured pretty girls with big smiles and long dark hair.

"No, Captain," Laura said. "But we'll keep an eye out for them. No luck so far?"

"Afraid not. Maybe they just went to the city for a trip or something. That's what we hope. That's probably what happened."

Laura nodded seriously. "Oh, Captain, have you seen Chloe and her kittens this morning?"

"Chloe had kittens? Well, I'll be. . . . No, can't say that we did, right, Tom?"

Sergeant Hannibal shook his head. "We'll keep an eye out."

"Thanks. Bye."

As Annie and Laura walked toward the river, Annie kept gazing at the photographs. "They're so pretty."

Laura nodded. "But not good enough."

Annie stopped walking. "What did you say?"

Laura's eyes flashed red and then returned to normal. Darker than normal, actually. She asked, "Did I just say something?"

Annie grunted. "Yes, and it wasn't nice. What do you mean they're not good enough? Good enough for what?"

Laura mocked Annie's concern. "Good enough for what? Good enough for what? I told you I hadn't realized I said something. I must have been thinking about something else. Come on."

Annie counted to five and followed Laura, struggling to keep anger from making her say something to Laura she'd regret. Annie decided to go with the flow and just act like a best friend to Laura. That might mean confronting her later, but right now the sun was shining, people were smiling, and Annie's crazy thoughts seemed just that. Crazy thoughts that weren't real. Annie couldn't do anything about it.

They were near the Mississippi River now. With her new attitude struggling to brighten her environment, Annie jumped into a rowboat tied to a big old round piling. The boat was one of dozens of rowboats and canoes owned by Midwest University for student use, and they were numbered Wildcat 1 through Wildcat 30-something. Annie felt playful, and when Laura stood away from the water's edge, Annie said, "Come on, let's take a spin." Annie flipped up the oarlocks and threaded the oars through the U-shaped locks.

Laura started walking away, but Annie got out of the boat and sneaked up behind Laura and dragged her back to the boat. Laura resisted fiercely, but Annie's muscles bulged and she knew it was no contest. She would get Laura into the boat. As she lifted the lighter girl over the gunwale, Annie realized Laura was sobbing.

Annie unclenched her arms. "What's the matter?"

Laura turned and gave Annie a hateful look. Annie was stunned and could feel her cheeks turning red from embarrassment.

"You know my skin is allergic to water," Laura sobbed. "What if the boat overturned, you idiot? I hate you! Why don't you just go home!"

Laura stomped off, leaving Annie to keep her balance in the gently rocking boat. Annie was certain that now she had really gone and lost her best friend for good. She slapped the water, disgusted with herself, and disgusted with Laura. Annie muttered under her breath about how crazy Laura had gotten, how crazily changed she was, and how insensitive Laura was about their friendship. Little things like this had never bothered Laura. In fact, she mostly laughed her big-roar laugh when they wrestled because it reminded them both of their first-grade fight. That memory shook Annie up. She had hoped to never lose Laura's friendship, and she felt miserable. Maybe she should go home. Laura wasn't being a very good friend. She seemed to think only of herself.

Annie jumped out of the boat to look for her buddy anyway. Her best buddy. Maybe. But if Laura didn't shape up soon, Annie didn't see how they could remain friends.

*　　*　　*

She found Laura brooding back at the house. Before Annie could say anything, Laura started crying and hugged Annie, telling her she was sorry again.

"My headaches are worse, Annie. What's happening to me?"

Annie didn't know what to say. This was the first time she had heard about headaches.

"What kind of headaches?"

"A big, constant headache," Laura sobbed, rubbing her forehead. "I've had it for a month, and it keeps getting worse."

"Did you tell your dad?" Annie asked. She was worried, but she wondered if Laura was putting her on. Laura was certainly riding an out-of-control roller coaster when it came to their friendship.

"Yeah, but he told me they would go away. They haven't. Because . . ." Laura stopped, but she stared at Annie, as if she wanted to tell her something.

"Because what?" Annie asked, impatient.

Laura shook her head and looked at the floor. She clutched a throw pillow to her stomach.

A strange thought popped into Annie's head. "Laura, does this have anything to do with my dream?"

Laura laughed, a scoffing laugh, and Annie was embarrassed and sorry that she had asked. But then Laura said something that made Annie even sorrier.

"You don't remember your dream," Laura said softly.

"Oh, yes, I do. It was a horrible dream. The mummy—a horrible, ugly thing when it moved—gave you a drink. And she talked about the kittens and their tails, and it grossed me out. It seemed so real—"

"The mummy isn't ugly, and you didn't have a dream," Laura said, a smile curling her lips, her voice getting even softer.

"Yes, I did. I just told you—what do you mean the mummy isn't ugly?"

"It was real, Annie."

A simple enough statement, Annie thought. *Simple enough to make me ready for the loony bin.* Now it was Annie's turn to smile. But hers was crooked. "You're teasing me, Laura. I thought we were best friends."

"We are best friends, you dolt. That's why they want us." Laura remained staring at Annie.

The hairs on the back of Annie's neck now permanently stuck out. Little cold bumps formed all over her body. She couldn't *not* ask.

"Who wants us?" Annie said, but her voice sounded different to her. It was cracking.

"Why, the mummies, of course. They're alive. And they want our bodies because . . . well, you wouldn't understand."

"Try me, Laura!" Annie yelled.

Laura shook her head. "Nope. There's only one way. I need to show you."

"No, no, no. I bet there are three or four different ways to tell me. You don't need to show me."

"I'm not sure what they want with us," Laura said. "But it can't be good. Maybe . . . maybe you should go home, Annie. They want both of us, so maybe this will all go away if you do."

Annie was too terrified to leave. She needed Laura right now, and Laura needed her. "I can't leave, Laura."

"Then swear you'll help me, Annie. Help us."

Annie crossed her heart, spooked beyond belief because Laura was so serious. "I swear," Annie squeaked. But she wanted to check the bus schedule.

"Good," Laura said. "We'll confront them tonight."

"Confront who?" Annie's teeth started chattering, and she thought it was absurd. They had buses leaving every day, right?

"The mummies, of course," Laura said. Then she cried, and Annie hugged her.

CHAPTER 5

Annie and Laura silently closed the D'Orricos' front door and stepped into the darkness. At a little after one in the morning, cold, blue moonlight cast the girls' shadows onto the creamy concrete sidewalk.

"Come on," Laura whispered, and the two friends rushed through the ghostly light, the tree branches waving leaves that rustled to make a soft, shimmering sound.

"You haven't told me anything!" Annie said to Laura's back. "I must be crazy to follow you!"

Laura just made a chopping motion with her hand, and Annie clenched her teeth. Laura hadn't said another thing about the mummies since her startling afternoon revelation, one which made Annie think Laura might be having some head problems. But Annie was worried about her own sanity, so she went along. She wanted answers, not mystery. No, check that—she wanted out of here.

At the science building, Laura unlocked the double doors with a set of jangling keys, and then she punched in the security code outside the lab. The door clicked open, and Laura pushed Annie through the opening and into the blackness of the unlit lab. It smelled musty. Very musty.

"Wait!" Annie whispered hoarsely. "I can't see a thing."

Laura pushed anyway, and Annie bumped into a chair.

"Ow!" she said, far too loud.

Both girls stood statue still, waiting to see if Annie's outburst attracted attention from . . . something.

"What's that?" Annie asked, and she clutched Laura's arm.

"What?" Laura asked.

"Do you hear breathing?" Annie gasped. She looked frantically around the room as she placed Laura protectively behind her.

"Of course I hear breathing, Annie. You're panting like Tommy Ward's old hound dog, and I'm breathing in your ear because you're squishing me."

Annie released her grip on Laura, glad that Laura couldn't see her crooked smile. She felt a little foolish, but the place really gave her the creeps.

Laura tugged on Annie's shirt bottom. "Come on, I want to show you something."

Laura slowly pulled Annie across the room, careful not to bang into furniture. Chairs from desks stuck out around the lab. The girls inched their way to the corner of the lab where the mummies' glass cases were safely tucked away. Low-level lighting from the temperature and humidity monitors reflected off the polished glass.

Finally Laura and Annie stood beside the cases.

"Well," Annie said, "what do we do now?"

She gazed around the lab, her eyes becoming accustomed to the darkness.

"Annie!" Laura suddenly screeched. "There's something wrong!"

Annie twirled and saw that Laura was staring at the glass cases. Annie focused her eyes to look inside the cases, and then she had to stifle her own scream.

The mummies were not in the cases!

"Where are they?" Annie asked.

"Look!" Laura said, and gasped.

Annie brought her eyes away from the cases to see where Laura pointed.

Annie took in a lungful of breath. There were hundreds of sets of pinpoint red eyes staring at them, and the sound of rustling feet made Annie sick. It was the sound she had heard in her dream—no, it hadn't been a dream. Rats had crawled over her face! These rats.

The eyes edged closer.

Laura grabbed Annie's arm as the rustling sound grew, and suddenly Annie was being dragged bodily by Laura through a rear door she had banged open. Annie heard hundreds of feet and tails scrambling behind them.

"Down this corridor!" Laura yelled, and Annie sprinted as fast as she could without running up Laura's back, which she wanted to do badly.

They were in a cement block corridor.

"This goes between the lab and the fieldhouse!" Laura

panted as she ran. Annie heard the rats squealing behind them, getting closer. Now they began nipping at her sneakers, jumping on her legs, and she ran faster, pushing Laura ahead, grabbing her by the shoulders so Laura wouldn't fall.

"Move it!" Annie screamed. The burst of speed gained them some ground.

Laura pulled Annie to the left as they came to a fork. This pathway was much narrower than the main corridor. The two girls pressed against the wall and didn't make a sound, although Annie blew gently to force a silky cobweb from sticking to her lips and face. The rats rushed by, continuing down the wide corridor.

Annie spotted a misty light near the end of the narrow corridor, and she heard low voices. Thank goodness. There were other people here. Maybe the rats would stay away.

As they neared the light, Annie could hear the voices more clearly, and it sounded like chanting. She was certain she had heard it before, like a song whose melody sticks to your brainpan.

Then Annie heard the voice speak English.

"Come, little kittens," the voice said. "We need those tender tails."

Annie remembered the voice, but the memory was unthinkable. The voice had been in her dream. The dream that Laura said Annie had never had. The dream that Laura said was a real event.

"Let's get out of here," Laura said.

Annie almost agreed, but what she had heard about

46

kitten tails affected her deeply. Could it be Chloe's kittens? And why would the woman need kitten tails?

"No," Annie said. "We've got to take a look. What if those are Chloe's kittens?"

"Come on, Annie. It's probably just someone who isn't sleepy. That room is underneath the laundry. So maybe someone is washing clothes and their cat chased a rat down here. Maybe that's all."

Annie frowned at Laura and said, "At one in the morning? That woman said she *needed cat tails.* Come on. Let's see."

Annie eased closer to the light, and then she stood up straight. Scurrying noises were rushing at them down the narrow corridor they had just traversed. The rats were back! The girls ran down the steps as the rats came flying into view. Annie and Laura tumbled through a doorway and into a searing hot room.

Annie untangled herself from Laura and stood, brushing a layer of chalky dust from her shorts and shirt. She looked up and wished she hadn't. She could not believe her eyes.

Candles burned everywhere, hundreds of candles that flickered as heat from the industrial dryers blew down through vents from the laundry room above. It was as dry as a desert in the room.

Then Annie noticed that in addition to lit candles, people flickered in the room. The two missing college girls—Annie recognized their faces from the photographs the campus police had handed out—leaned back with their arms crossed, their bodies upright in makeshift sarcophaguses. Both of the girls were unconscious or sleeping, and their arms were multicolored, much like Laura's. They looked somehow transformed. Much like Laura.

Worse, set atop a metal shelf rack, Chloe's kittens struggled to force their way out of a cruel iron mesh cage. The kittens were crying, mewling to Annie, pleading with her. Chloe was also in the cage, her back arched, but Chloe wasn't looking at Annie and Laura.

Annie followed Chloe's gaze, and what she saw froze her and horrified her. The two mummies, the gruesome evil things dead for five thousand years, stood opposite them. Both mummies smiled at Annie and Laura with grotesque skeletal grins, their yellowed teeth the focal point of their hideous heads.

The mummy from Annie's dream opened her mouth to speak, and saliva strands wobbled as she said, "Welcome, my little pathways."

Annie automatically started to back away, pulling Laura with her, but Laura resisted, staring at the mummies, ignoring Annie.

Annie pulled Laura away and turned to run up the stairs, but a loud hiss stopped her in her tracks.

Two feet away was the largest snake Annie had ever seen. It raised itself on its tubular body, and as it reared up, a hood blossomed around the open mouth that sprouted two spike-size fangs, and Annie knew she faced a cobra. The green, scaly nightmare held Annie immobile.

Annie fought a wave of dizziness, but she lost the battle and fell back onto Laura. Laura caught her, and Annie blacked out for the second time on her trip.

CHAPTER
6

Annie woke, a stinging sensation burning behind her eyes. Just as she tried to open her eyes, a thin bony hand with grotesque curved nails made gentle contact just under her left cheekbone.

"Hey!" Annie yelled. "Let go!"

"Wake up, my pathway," the mummy witch said, her teeth pointing at Annie. She stared at Annie, and her eyes were so . . . powerful. Annie was compelled to hold her gaze. It felt good, right, that she listen to the . . . eyes. Annie felt a calm wash over her and she took stock of her surroundings.

Annie sat in a folding chair, but she wasn't bound to it by rope as she expected. Instead, the witch had mesmerized her. She knew so intuitively. She couldn't run if she wanted to. And she realized she didn't want to run. Something weird bubbled below the surface of her mind, but right now she felt so comfortable.

Annie gazed to her right and saw Laura sitting beside her, a very dazed Laura. Laura appeared to be sitting there. It made Annie confused, and then angry.

"You led me here, Laura," she accused her friend.

Laura shrugged and said, "I tried to get you to go home, but you wouldn't listen. I really tried, Annie. But she was too strong for me. They won."

Not looking at the witch anymore, Annie felt her own consciousness returning, stoked by the anger.

"Look at me!" the witch demanded, but Annie closed her eyes.

Annie had always felt that an offense was the best form of defense, and now was as good a time as any because the mesmerizing hold of the witch was fading without eye contact. Annie looked up at Laura and said sarcastically, and with a bit more bravery than she actually felt, "You think these two refugees from a bad embalming experience won? Won what? They lost five thousand years ago. Your dad said so—"

"You foolish little girl," the head witch said. "Laura understands. But you won't, until it's too late. I said look at me!"

"And what, Miss Ugly," Annie taunted, staring at the ground, "does Laura understand? That you smell like a sack of wet newspapers? That linen bandages went out of fashion a few thousand years ago? That—"

Annie's tirade was interrupted by Laura's loud laugh, which made everyone jump, and the witch stepped back

50

a bit. Annie glanced at Laura, still laughing, and quickly said, "That you're about fifty centuries late for a badly needed dental cleaning? Look at those teeth. I've seen better teeth on old horses. In fact—"

"Enough!" the witch screamed. She moved her face to within an inch of Annie's nose, and then she reached behind her and grabbed a glass beaker filled with smoky blue liquid. It appeared to be the same shade as the stuff Laura drank in Annie's dream—no, not a dream, a real event, Annie corrected herself. Annie leaned away from the beaker as the witch brought it close to Annie's lips. The potion smelled terrible. It made Annie recall the time a skunk got caught inside their garbage can for a couple of days. The combination of rotting garbage and the scent of frustrated skunk who had sprayed all over the inside of the can had been horrible, but this potion smelled worse. Annie smacked her lips shut and turned her head aside.

"Come, Annie," the witch said nicely this time. "We've made this especially for you. It won't hurt at all. I promise you."

Annie opened her mouth briefly to say, "You got that right, witch. That stuff isn't touching my lips."

"It's not supposed to, dearie," the witch responded. "It's supposed to travel down your gullet to your stomach, where it can begin working your wondrous transformation. Soon you'll be my best friend."

The second witch cackled, her teeth clacking nastily.

"What transformation?" Annie asked.

"Laura knows—right, Laura?" the witch asked.

Laura nodded in resignation.

"Let me go," Annie demanded. "Let *us* go—or you'll be sorry." Annie stared defiantly, and the witch caught her gaze, and Annie immediately felt the power again. She tried to tear her eyes away. She couldn't believe she was talking to a long-dead mummy. If this was a dream or hallucination, and Annie hoped it was, she certainly wanted to control her part in it. But she knew it wasn't. However, taunting these ugly things seemed to make them talk about their plans. And Annie wanted to know what was in store so she could devise an escape. She wouldn't go easily.

"And another thing," Annic said. "Look at those nails. Nobody wears their nails like that anymore. You need a manicure. But the manicurist would need a chainsaw, or an ax, and maybe she could cut that ugly head off that geek's pencil-neck while she's at it—"

Laura honked a loud laugh, and the witch holding Annie started again, glancing at Laura, and Annie made her move. She pushed up to knock the potion out of the witch's hand, but the witch was terribly fast and pulled the beaker back. Annie opened her mouth in surprise, and with a lightning-quick motion, the witch hurled the contents of the beaker toward Annie's face. Before Annie could put up a hand, half the liquid came flying out in a splash, and Annie swallowed a lot of the nasty-smelling stuff before she knew what had happened. The taste was revolting, and Annie started gagging immediately. Standing now, she looked about and then ran to a janitor's messy sink.

Annie turned on the water and the witch screamed, *"No!* No water!!"

Annie washed her mouth out, spitting out the vile blue liquid, but she feared she had swallowed too much.

"Get her!" the head witch screamed, and both witches pounced at Annie.

Annie remembered Laura's burning arm, and now this witch screamed something about no water. Reacting, Annie scooped water out of the sink and tossed it at the charging witches, who pulled up short as the water splashed them. When the water made contact, the witches screamed, and where the water hit the linen bandages, small puffs of smoke rose up with a *pooosh* sound, and the witches shrank back. Annie wondered why the smoke was in small poofs, unlike the billowing smoke Annie had seen rise from Laura's skin during the laundry incident. She filed that information away, however, when she saw that Laura had stood and was peering around wide-eyed.

"Laura!" Annie yelled. "Come on!"

Annie looked up and saw the cage holding Chloe and the kittens. She unlatched the cage, and Chloe jumped out, hissing, her back arched like a mountain peak, and the massive cobra, about to lunge at Annie, slid back to protect itself from Chloe's swiping paws.

Annie grabbed the cage with the kittens and shouted, "Laura, come on!"

Annie raced to the corridor, hoping Laura would follow, and she took the steps two at a time, uncaring about the puny vermin now. She heard Chloe hissing behind her, and the rats squealing as they tried to flee Chloe's rage.

Annie flew through the door to the cool outside, and

53

Chloe raced out after her. Annie set the cage down and freed the kittens. Chloe and the kittens ran off into the night, and Annie swore she saw Chloe smile at her before she bounded after her kittens, who raced haphazardly across the grass.

Annie took a deep breath. Should she go back to get Laura? She steeled herself, and just as she opened the door, Laura tumbled out.

"Run!" Laura screamed. "They're right behind me!"

Laura took off after the kittens.

The door banged open again, and the two mummies raced outside. The head mummy took off after Laura, and Annie raced the other way, the second mummy in pursuit.

Annie liked to run, but not with something horrible chasing behind. She pumped her arms and legs faster than she had ever done before, panting, taking in deep gulps of air, certain she had left the mummy in the dust. She slowed a bit to conserve her strength, taking deep breaths through her nostrils. The clean night air smelled wonderful.

Suddenly Annie gagged. The clean night smell turned musty, like wet newspapers that had dried. She looked behind her and saw a blurred bundle of rags about to grab her shoulder.

Annie kicked into high gear again and ran toward the Olympic Swimming and Diving Complex on the other side of the gym. The wind had picked up. Swaying tree branches distracted her as she ran, the wind blowing into her face. A storm was brewing.

Annie smelled the musty scent again and looked back

over her shoulder. The mummy was gaining again, but Annie almost stopped when she glanced at the mummy's face. She thought she was looking in a mirror. The mummy's face resembled Annie's to a scary degree. Annie looked ahead, concentrating on running hard. Sweat poured off her brow and into her eyes, the salt stinging and making her blink. She wiped her eyes with her arm, and she gagged again, the musty scent back, and when she looked at her arm under the cold moonlight, she saw that it had turned coppery brown, just as Laura's arm had.

She was confused, and then she felt terrified as she realized that the musty smell was coming from her own body. She was being transformed into the witch who was chasing her! And the closer the witch got, the faster Annie changed. Annie was almost out of energy, but she charged ahead, more afraid of the mummy and what she would do to Annie than of running out of breath.

A chain-link fence loomed in front of Annie. The fence surrounded the pool complex. Annie jumped high when she reached the fence, clawing at the links to get a climbing grip. Tired beyond belief, she forced herself to scale the fence, scrambling with her arms and legs to climb the eight-foot wall of crisscrossed iron wire. Just as she reached the top, she felt a tug on her sneaker. She was caught in one of the iron diamonds formed by the crossing wires. Annie looked down to free her foot, and she almost screamed. She was *not* caught in a chain link.

The witch, halfway up the fence, had grabbed Annie's sneaker, and now she was using her other arm to grab

Annie's calf. Annie watched, stunned, as her leg began to turn coppery brown, spreading up from the witch's grasp. Annie pulled her leg as hard as she could, and she felt her sneaker give way.

Soundlessly the witch dropped to the ground, one hand still holding Annie's sneaker. Annie scrambled up and over the fence. She turned and looked through the fence to see where the witch had gone, but the witch was not on the ground. Weird. Annie heard a cackle and looked up. The witch was atop the chain-link fence, about to pounce on Annie. She couldn't understand how the witch had recovered so fast, but she didn't wait to ask. She started running again.

Annie looked back and saw that the witch was right behind her, but she looked even more like Annie now, her hair blondish, and Annie feared it was all over. But she wouldn't give up. She stumbled as the grass turned into the concrete apron of the Olympic diving pool. She had almost regained her footing when her sneakerless foot caught on a crack between two concrete slabs. Annie tripped and fell headlong into the pool.

The water revived her, its coolness a blessing, but suddenly Annie heard a splash. The witch had dived into the pool after her. Annie started swimming, almost completely out of energy, her lungs screaming, her muscles refusing to do what her brain ordered, and then the worst burning sensation Annie had ever felt assaulted her skin all over. Annie's dark coppery skin was smoking in great billows, the water hissing all around her. Just before she panicked, the unbearable pain lessened as the smoke diminished. Annie treaded water, and saw that her arm had changed back to her own skin color, and that the pain was wafting away with the smoke that drifted up and across the full leathery moon. But across the pool, the mummy wasn't doing as well.

The smoke surrounding the witch was growing in intensity every second, and she screamed shrilly, flailing her arms in the water, thrashing around as it she were being eaten by a great white shark. Annie saw that the mummy's face was reverting to its old ugly self, and the oval mouth that was screaming was doing so with its own yellowed buck teeth, and not Annie's pearly whites. Annie felt her face, and happily ran her fingers over familiar features. Whatever had just happened between Annie and the witch and the blue potion, Annie had her body back, and the witch was burning and smoking in the water. *Of course,* Annie thought, *that's it! Lots and lots of water hurt the witches.* Annie gazed at the witch, who was struggling to get out of the pool, her arms on the concrete, inching her body out.

Annie swam to the witch, determined to make sure that she didn't get out of the pool. She reached the witch just as the ugly mummy had pulled her upper body out of the water, still smoking, still screaming.

Annie threw her arms around the witch's legs as the limbs were kicking out of the pool. Annie scissored her own legs to tread water, and she tried to pull the witch back into the pool, back into the water and ultimate destruction.

The witch intensified her struggle, thrashing with a terrible determination, lashing out at Annie, but Annie had the upper hand and wouldn't let go. Smoke hissed out of the water, which was now bubbling all around Annie, but still she held on. The water was heating up, burning, and abruptly the witch let out a horrific scream which seemed to last half a minute.

Suddenly there was no more struggle, and Annie was thrown back in the pool. It was as if the witch had been a rubber band that had snapped. Annie knew she had won because she still held on to something. When she surfaced, Annie looked at her arms. She was holding nothing but bandages. Sparkling clean bandages. But then she heard the scream of the witch.

Annie looked up and saw the witch, or half of her, upright on her arms and knuckles on the concrete slab surrounding the pool, swaying like a gorilla. Annie looked at the clean linen in her hands and realized that the witch's legs had dissolved completely in the water, leaving only bandages.

The witch screamed once more and turned about on her knuckles. Legless, she scampered away on her arms like some grotesque chimpanzee.

Annie pulled herself out of the pool and watched, stunned, as the hideous, legless thing crawled over the fence and loped away across the grass.

Annie stood. Shocked, she knew she had to get moving. Laura needed her help. And she had a lot of explaining to do.

CHAPTER
7

Annie raced to the D'Orrico home. Laura had headed there with the lead witch in hot pursuit. A jagged neon white bolt jumped in front of Annie, startling her, and the crack of thunder followed immediately. Raindrops the size of Ping-Pong balls splattered on the sidewalk around Annie, and then the heavenly waters ripped through the clouds. Annie, still wet from the pool, welcomed the rain. Since the mummies seemed to hate water, they wouldn't venture out in this weather. She hoped Laura had made it back. Annie jogged to the house, looking cautiously about as she ran.

The D'Orricos' front door was wide open when Annie arrived.

The house was in complete darkness.

Annie tiptoed through the front door. The moon had disappeared behind the storm clouds, so Annie let her eyes adjust to the interior darkness. She was spooked. What if the mummy had followed Laura back here? What if the mummy was in the house right now? Annie took a deep breath to calm her rising adrenaline rush, and then she smiled and let her shoulders sag when she heard the meow of one of the kittens. Annie closed the front door and locked it.

Annie bent down and the kitten ran around her hands and legs a few times before stopping and leaning into Annie. Annie scooped the little gray softness into her hands and walked to the bedroom.

"Laura?" she called softly.

No answer.

Annie went to the lower bunk. Something was bunched in a ball beneath the covers. Annie pulled them back and saw Laura—sleeping.

Annie shook Laura gently, and Laura's eyes opened abruptly. Laura glared at Annie for a few seconds. Her eyes softened and she extended her legs. Then she stretched her arms by raising them over her head.

"Annie?"

"Who else?" Annie replied, stroking the kitten's back.

"Eww . . . get that cat out of here!" Laura hissed. "Now."

"Forget it. What happened to you?" Annie asked, concerned about Laura, concerned about the insanity of tonight's events. Laura was worried about a cat?

"It was horrible," Laura whispered. "Bring the kitten to Chloe downstairs, and I'll tell you. I don't want my skin aggravated, Annie. Do it now."

Annie backed off, thinking that Laura must be

stressed, too. She brought the little gray to the basement stairs and called for Chloe. Chloe bounded up the steps and began licking the kitten, and Annie saw that Chloe had a scratched nose which was crusting over.

"Oh, you poor thing," Annie said as she stroked Chloe's back firmly. Chloe meowed and then prodded the kitten downstairs.

Annie went back to the room and sat on Laura's bed. She had to shake Laura awake again. Annie couldn't believe Laura had fallen back to sleep.

"I'm tired, that's why," Laura said when Annie looked at her funny. "You want to know why I fell asleep. I don't know. I ran home so fast I couldn't believe it. I'm exhausted," Laura said. "What happened to you?"

Annie said, "I'm okay. It was close, but I think I found a way to destroy the mummies."

"Oh, yeah?" Laura asked, her eyebrows hitching. "How?"

"I'll tell you in a minute. But are you all right? Laura, what's happening? I'm scared out of my mind. Is this real? Are we having a bad dream?"

"It's real, Annie," Laura replied. "Too real. I can't explain it. Things we can't even imagine are just happening, and we need help."

"I agree with my whole heart," Annie said. "Somebody's got to do something. These mummies are seriously evil things."

"Oh, Annie," Laura said. "I didn't want to believe it at first. Strange things have been happening ever since the mummies arrived in their crates. I tried to tell my dad, but he just acted like I was pulling his leg. People

61

will think we're crazy if we tell them about the mummies."

Annie nodded and said, "You're right, but I don't care what they think of me. These two witches need to be stopped before they hurt us. Why are they doing this? What do they hope to gain?"

"Annie, they told us that tonight. Don't you see? They're trying to take us over. Their minds will be in our bodies, and that will let them tell lies like crazy when they get to the Next World. They need us for one thing, and one thing only—our hearts. According to them, our hearts are as light as feathers, and they think they'll fool those Assessor things when our hearts are weighed instead of their real heavy evil ones."

"Well, fine, but if they take our bodies over, what happens to us? I mean, our minds. Where do our minds go?"

"You don't want to know," Laura said.

"I always want to know where I'm going," Annie said, and she fixed her gaze on Laura to let her know she wasn't kidding. Laura didn't laugh.

"We become the mummies and go back to sleep, where we'll be in a museum for eternity. And the worst part is, I think we'll know it. We'll be watching people from all over the world stare at us. We'll be museum exhibits."

"No way," Annie said. "No way."

"Annie, we lost. They made us drink the potion. I tried so hard to fight it, but I'm almost there. I wanted you to go home, and now you're almost there . . . hey, what happened to you? How come you're not transformed?"

"That's what I tried to tell you earlier . . . I think I found the answer—"

"Hey, what are you two doing up?" Dr. D'Orrico said, peeking his head in the room. "It's past 2 A.M."

"Sorry, Dad," Laura said. "Annie's keeping me up with some ghost stories."

"What?" Annie blurted, surprised. "Let's tell him, Laura."

"Tell me what?"

Laura glared at Annie. She appeared to be struggling, fighting herself. "Nothing, Dad. Really."

"It's not nothing, Dr. D'Orrico. Something terrible is happening to me and Laura."

"What?" Dr. D'Orrico asked, intrigued. He stepped into the room.

"Yeah, Dad," Laura said. "Our friendship is heading for the rocks."

"What?" Annie and Dr. D'Orrico asked at the same time.

"That's right, Dad. But we're working it out."

"That's good," Dr. D'Orrico said, shaking his head, frowning at the girls. "Now go to sleep. Talk it out in the morning."

"But . . . but Dr. D'Orrico," Annie said, "that's not it at all. You see, it's about your mummies. They're alive, and they're trying to take over Laura's body and my body—"

Laura boomed one of the loudest laughs she had ever unleashed in Annie's presence, making Dr. D'Orrico jump, and scaring Annie so much that she banged her head on the top bunk.

"See what I mean, Dad?" Laura gasped between harsh laughs. "I told her those things I told you a while back, and now she's pulling your leg."

"Annie Carr, you sly thing." Dr. D'Orrico chuckled. "I see. First Laura concocted that crazy story, and she kept bugging me about it. She was trying to get me to spend more time with her by making these silly things up. Now she's got you doing it, too. No more pranks, girls. I promise we'll do something special as soon as the mummies are on their way back to Egypt. Now get to sleep. I mean it."

Dr. D'Orrico closed the bedroom door, and the girls heard him slap his bare feet on the wooden floor as he headed back to his own room.

"Laura! Why did you do that!" Annie demanded, extremely upset. "We have no credibility now!"

"Annie, dear, I told you that my father thinks the mummy stories are a prank! He didn't listen to me. Why did you think he'd believe you?"

Annie sighed disgustedly. "Well, what we went through tonight was real. Much too real for me. Somebody ought to listen. We're not crazy." Annie recalled the horrible scene in the basement room below the laundry at the fieldhouse. But of course, she thought. "Laura, we saw those missing college girls."

"So what?" Laura asked.

"So, who else is looking for them?"

"Everybody."

"That's right," Annie replied. "Especially those police officers."

"What are you suggesting?"

"Let's go to the police station right now and bring them to the room! Maybe we'll catch the witches in the act. We can free the college girls, and then the police will have to believe us."

"Go there at two in the morning? I'm exhausted. Why not wait until the morning. It's only a few hours away. Besides, I'm not going to walk across campus at night with those mummies still around."

"But—" Annie said, about to tell Laura why the rain would keep the mummies inside, but she saw that the rain had stopped. The storm had blown through quickly.

"But nothing," Laura said with a yawn. "I'm asleep."

Annie opened her mouth to speak, but Laura was snoring. How did she do that?

Annie settled into bed, and she made herself not think about things. Images of the college girls danced in her mind, and Annie knew she couldn't wait until morning to go back. She'd close her eyes for five minutes and calm down, and then she'd wake Laura and force her to go to the police station with her. Everything would be all right.

Four hours later, at 5 A.M., Annie awoke with a start. It had been more than a nap. She thought of the college girls imprisoned in the sarcophaguses, and weird feelings flooded her insides. She had let them down. Annie hoped it wasn't too late. She hopped down from the top bunk and turned on the overhead light. She skipped back to the bed and shook Laura awake. Laura glared at

65

Annie, and her eyes flashed a nasty look, but then softened. Annie thought Laura's eyes looked darker.

"Come on," Annie said. "We've got to get to the police station."

"Wait a minute," Laura replied, raising her arms until they reached the top bunk. Laura grasped the mattress slats of the upper bunk and began stretching.

"Do you ache?" Annie asked. "I do. I haven't had a workout like last night since soccer ended. Of course, the stakes were never so high. I'd rather have a crazy Jeannie Reilly chase me down a soccer field than have that Rat Witch grabbing my ankles. Let's go, Laura!"

Laura scrunched up her face and said, "It's not even dawn yet. I'm hungry. Let's eat."

"After the police station! Come on, Laura, those girls need our help!"

Laura shook her head and shrugged. "And what do we tell the police? What if nobody's in that room? We need time to think about this."

"Think about what? Think about what? Get a move on, Laura!"

Laura sat up and swung her legs over the side of the bed.

"See you in a few. I'll get ready first."

"Laura!" Annie whispered hoarsely. She didn't want to wake Dr. D'Orrico.

"Toodle-oo," Laura said. She walked slowly out of the bedroom.

Annie fumed as she dressed. She went to the kitchen and pulled a cereal box from the pantry, filling two bowls and adding milk to hers. Annie chewed her cereal so hard she ground her teeth, wondering what to do about Laura. She hadn't seemed concerned about the girls at all. Annie heard footsteps heading toward the kitchen and turned to scold Laura.

Dr. D'Orrico stood in the doorway, scratching his head, his hair sticking out at odd angles.

"Annie," he stated. "What's going on?"

"Oh, hi, Dr. D'Orrico. Laura and I are getting an early start."

"I'll say."

Dr. D'Orrico fetched a bowl and filled it with cereal.

"What do you two have planned?" he asked, a mouthful of milk and oats adding mumbles to his question.

"We're going to take the bus into town," Laura said. She appeared at the table in her bathrobe, her hair in a towel. She looked refreshed and confident, as if nothing had happened last night. Annie froze, confused, a spoonful of cereal hovering with a shake near her open mouth.

"Watch out for flies, Annie," Laura said, and honked a laugh much too loud as the sun streamed through the window to announce the dawn.

Annie said, "I thought we were going to visit the museum—near the campus police station." Annie raised her eyebrows, looking for agreement from Laura.

"Later," Laura said nonchalantly. "After we shop. I need a new dress."

"Another dress?" Dr. D'Orrico asked, smiling. "My little girl is growing up."

"Oh, be quiet, Dad. It's not as if you care. You're a workaholic. Go to work." Laura frowned at her dad.

"I see," Dr. D'Orrico replied. He hung his head, then

67

stood and placed his half-eaten bowl of cereal in the sink. As he walked through the door, he grabbed the molding and turned. He looked very sad. "Enjoy yourselves, girls. I'll see you tonight."

"Thank you, sir," Annie said, and then glared at Laura, who shrugged and ignored her father's stare. Dr. D'Orrico winced and left.

"What's that about, best friend?" Annie asked.

"It's about time," Laura answered sarcastically. "You're no help. 'Thank you, sir'—blah, blah, blah. Keep it to yourself."

Annie bit her tongue and said icily, "I'm not going shopping. I'm visiting the police."

"You don't have a strategy. They'll think you're nuts."

"Not if you come with me and say the same thing."

Annie set her mouth in a straight line. Laura had gone over the edge again, unhappy about her father. But Annie wondered what else was going on. Laura had resisted going to the police last night, and now she was pulling the same stunt.

"What's the deal, Laura?"

"The deal, 'best friend,' is that we go shopping in town and discuss what to say. Then, if you want, we'll go to the police. Things about last night are a little foggy in my mind."

"Oh," Annie replied. "I think things are foggy, all right. The fog seems to be blowing out of your ear."

Laura smiled at Annie. "You see, but you don't understand." She snorted.

Annie wanted to cry, but her anger and her pride kept her impassive. She decided to play Laura's game, whatever it was. She really had no choice. She needed Laura to provide substance to the crazy story they had to tell the police. She couldn't do it alone. After all, Laura had gotten her into this.

"I know," Annie said, "that no matter how bad you treat me or your father, we both still like you. But maybe not for long."

"Annie my dear, we're going to be best friends forever. Don't forget it." Laura's eyes flashed darkly again, and then she stood and left the room.

Annie looked at her cereal and threw her spoon down. She wasn't hungry anymore.

Annie suffered through three hours of shopping, not speaking, wanting to shake some sense into Laura, but she couldn't very well drag her to the police station. Laura was stonewalling, and only Laura knew why. Annie felt powerless to do anything. If Laura wanted to act this way, Annie couldn't do anything about it. Some friend.

Finally, after a silent fast-food lunch, Laura said, "Let's go to the police station."

"We didn't discuss what we're going to say," Annie stated, but it was a question.

Laura smiled sarcastically and said, "Well, best friend, you seem so anxious to make us look like fools, and you're so sure of yourself. You can do all the talking."

Annie fumed at Laura. Sure of herself? Not really. Scared to death. Annie wrapped her garbage and threw it in the waste can. She turned to Laura and said, *"My* best friend always helped me. *My* best friend was always a friend, not a sarcastic witch."

Laura's eyes flashed meanly, but then she regained her composure and shrugged, on the verge of tears. "And you took a lot, but you never really gave much. I called you. I wrote to you. I invited you. You expect things, Annie, but you don't do anything about problems except whine about poor Annie." Laura was crying now, and Annie felt her cheeks reddening. Laura added, "Your best friend will accompany you to the police station now."

Annie was numb. Laura's words stung deeply. How could Laura feel that way?

They made it to the station in fifteen minutes, and the captain and the sergeant politely escorted them into a conference room and offered them doughnuts when the girls confided they knew something about the missing college girls. Annie sat in a chair. Laura walked behind Annie and leaned against the wall, looking as if she wanted no part of the meeting.

"You do, do you?" asked Captain Cappello. He glanced at Sergeant Hannibal, gave him a knowing look, and turned back to the girls with a pained expression. "What do you know, Annie? It's Annie Carr, right?"

"Yes, sir, Captain," Annie replied, becoming very serious. She was nervous, having second thoughts about telling these two big men about the mummies. The story seemed so foolish now that she had to put it into words.

"Those girls," Annie said, "are being held captive near the laundry by Dr. D'Orrico's mummies."

Captain Cappello raised both eyebrows and then frowned. He became angry and said, "You know, we don't have time for jokes."

"It's no joke, Captain. We saw them last night. I'm telling the truth."

"The mummies came back to life, Annie?" asked Sergeant Hannibal. He looked at her kindly. "Maybe they just looked like the mummies. Ugly, were they?"

"Yes, sir, Sergeant. But they were live mummies. They said the curse was removed when they were brought from the tombs. And they want to take—"

"Annie," Sergeant Hannibal asked, looking past Annie's shoulder at Laura and squinting. "Do you read scary stories?"

Annie almost answered him, but clamped her mouth shut when she realized what was happening. She turned abruptly and caught Laura pointing at her temple and making a small circle with her index finger.

"I'm not crazy!" Annie screamed. "Laura, how could you!"

Laura opened her eyes wide and gave Annie a cruel look. Annie stared at her best friend, noticing that Laura's normally light brown eyes were now as black as coal. Suddenly Laura's behavior last night at home and while shopping this morning all made sense. It wasn't Laura. It was the head witch! Laura had been transformed! Annie held her breath, worried the witch—in Laura's body—knew what Annie was thinking. It was probably too late. The witch must have engineered this meeting to let the police think Annie was crazy. And maybe Annie *was* nuts.

"Annie?" Sergeant Hannibal asked. "Annie?"

"Huh?" she asked, turning around. She didn't want to turn her back to the witch, but everything was in slow

71

motion right then. Annie was going on instinct. But she had one goal. She didn't know how to do it, but she wanted her best friend back. And that meant defeating this witch behind her.

"Annie, let's try something different," Captain Cappello said. "Where did you see the girls?"

"At the fieldhouse, in a hidden room."

Captain Cappello looked from Sergeant Hannibal to Laura and then to Annie. "Do you think you can find this hidden room again?"

"Sure," Annie said. She looked at the witch. Although she wanted to shout, she said sweetly, "Right, Laura?"

"If you say so, Annie."

"Let's go," Captain Cappello said, donning his hat.

It was a short walk. As they made it down the deserted corridor, Annie kept up a stream of dialogue, telling the police about the rats and the cobra, and how scared they had been. She even told them about the chase the night before, and how the mummy had lost its legs in the pool. Captain Cappello said a few "Uh-huhs" as they walked along.

"Here," Annie said, and stopped outside the door. It was covered with cobwebs and looked as if it hadn't been opened in months.

Captain Cappello opened the door and pointed his flashlight about the room. "My goodness," he said.

"They're there?" Annie asked excitedly.

Captain Cappello motioned for Annie, Sergeant Hannibal, and "Laura" to enter. Annie pushed past, looked into the room, and saw—absolutely nothing. The place was completely deserted. Cobwebs and dust swirled in the beams of the flashlights as the officers crisscrossed the room.

"Rats might have been here," Sergeant Hannibal said, shining his light on the floor. "But that's about it. You have some explaining to do, Annie."

Annie just stood with her mouth open, the color draining from her face. It wouldn't do any good to say anything. Laura—the witch, actually—smiled at her and shrugged. Annie closed her eyes and started thinking, but she felt pretty hopeless.

"Come on, girls," Captain Cappello said. "I think Dr. D'Orrico needs to be told a few things. This is a serious matter. I'm disappointed by your prank. I'm sure Dr. D'Orrico will be disappointed—and embarrassed."

No one said a word on the way to the lab. And Dr. D'Orrico listened impassively while the captain quickly reviewed Annie's "prank."

"How could you girls do this?" Dr. D'Orrico asked, throwing his hands in the air. "Misleading these officers about those girls everyone is attempting to find—"

"Not attempting anymore, Doctor," Captain Cappello said. "We found the missing girls this morning. They were wandering around in a daze, uncertain where they'd been. We think they just don't want to tell us. A little amnesia, if you know what I mean. Their parents are coming to pick them up. Besides the crazy mummy angle, that's how we knew Annie was pulling a prank."

Annie was shocked. The mummies had set the college girls free?

"Laura," Captain Cappello concluded, "kept her wits

about her. She didn't appear to take any part in the charade. I'm afraid Annie is to blame."

Annie was dying inside. "Laura" had been right. No one believed her.

Dr. D'Orrico looked pained. "I don't understand. This is totally unlike Annie."

Annie hung her head, knowing it would be futile to protest.

"Captain, one of the mummies was vandalized last night. Its lower legs are missing. Only these clean bandages were left in place. Annie—and Laura—did you have anything to do with this?"

Annie was about to tell the truth, that she indeed had caused the mummy to lose its legs, but she stopped herself.

"No, Dr. D'Orrico. And I'm sorry about the story. At first I thought it was funny, but now I see how irresponsible I was." Annie glanced at "Laura" and saw her smile and nod.

"Your apology is accepted, Annie. But I'm afraid I must tell your parents. And you must go home."

Annie started crying, and "Laura" suddenly looked surprised. Annie looked at "Laura" through her tears, and she knew why the witch had panicked. She still needed Annie's body. But Annie had no intention of going anywhere without attempting to get her best friend back. Annie got ready to run, when "Laura" suddenly took charge, enabling Annie to stay.

"Dad!" "Laura" said. "Wait!" She looked around wildly, and then she resumed speaking. "It was my fault, Dad. I put Annie up to it. Said I wouldn't be her friend anymore unless she helped me get you away from your work. You work too much, Dad. But don't blame Annie. She's my . . . best friend."

Annie was sickened by the witch's smile, particularly since it was on Laura's face.

"Is that true, Annie?" Dr. D'Orrico asked sternly.

Annie said icily, "I'm afraid that what Laura said is true. I still feel bad."

"Captain," Dr. D'Orrico asked, "will you let me handle this? We're all very sorry that you and Sergeant Hannibal had to waste valuable time running this down. I assure you that these girls will be dealt with appropriately."

"Of course, Doctor." Captain Cappello and Sergeant Hannibal left without another word, but they did send disapproving glances the girls' way.

When they were alone, Dr. D'Orrico held up a hand before either girl could speak.

"Annie and Laura, that was an idiotic stunt. Laura, if you want more of my attention, this is not the way to go about it. If you want respect, you must earn it, not demand it. Until I determine an appropriate punishment, consider yourselves grounded."

Laura and Annie both apologized.

"Now go home, girls. Laura—I . . . understand why, but I strongly disapprove of your actions. I love you both. Let's rebuild from here. And think about what you can do to make things up to the captain and the sergeant."

The girls left the lab.

Outside, "Laura" turned to Annie and said menacingly, "That was close. But no more trouble from you. I'll be watching your every move. I don't sleep. Tonight we finish things."

Annie fell into step beside "Laura." She looked over and vowed to herself, *That's right, witch. Tonight we finish things. I want my friend back.*

Annie was wakened by a rude hand. She saw with one blurry eye that it was just past midnight. Annie opened her other eye and saw "Laura," smiled, and then recalled with horror that "Laura" was the head Rat Witch.

"Get dressed," the witch said. She threw Annie a wrinkled shirt and a pair of shorts. Annie dressed while she kept the witch in her sight. She smiled at the witch.

"Oh, you're pleased now?" the witch asked sarcastically, and Annie nodded. It was weird to see Laura's face and body, knowing it was inhabited by the witch.

"Why?"

Annie shrugged. "I'm nervous." *But not why you think I am, witch,* she thought. In fact, Annie felt almost helpless. But she had a tiny glimmer of confidence because Annie had learned something about herself, something she wouldn't let the witch know, and something that might not even matter to anyone—except Laura.

Annie had plotted all afternoon and into the night while she and the witch had parked themselves in front of the television. At first Annie had spent the afternoon hours feeling sorry for herself. The more she felt sorry for herself, the angrier she became. Angry at Laura for not telling her earlier about the witches, angry at Laura for not fighting the witches harder. And even though he was a nice man, Annie was angry at Dr. D'Orrico for moving here in the first place. Plus, as she thought about it, she was angry at him for not believing Laura and for not believing her. After pummeling Dr. D'Orrico in her mind's eye, Annie had brooded about Captain Cappello and Sergeant Hannibal. Why, they were supposed to protect and serve, but they only protected and served those witch mummies, without even realizing it.

After she had understood her anger wasn't helping anything, Annie spent a few hours doing superstitious things to help her wishes come true. She had held her breath during the commercials, telling herself that if she could last through three of them, then everything would work out all right, that Captain Cappello would come to his senses and realize Annie was the type of person never to lie about such serious matters.

When the show came back on, she counted to a thousand as fast as she could, thinking that if she made it to a thousand before the next set of commercials, then Sergeant Hannibal would come out and confront the witch.

Nothing had happened, so she tried completing her multiplication tables in her head up to ten times twenty before the witch spoke to her, hoping that Dr. D'Orrico would come home and see that "Laura" wasn't his daughter but was really the Rat Witch Mummy, but the witch had asked her for the clicker before she even got to nine times twelve.

Nothing was working.

So Annie went back to feeling sorry for herself, thinking that she had lost her best friend, that everyone was against her, that nobody would save her—or Laura. Laura couldn't save her—she had already been transformed into the Rat Witch. So Annie became angry at Laura once more, and that allowed her to get angry at everyone else again.

It was during the six o'clock news that it dawned on Annie that wishful thinking wasn't the way to make things happen. One of the news items featured a controversy at a local elementary school concerning how kids' math scores had gone down ever since the school board adopted a "new" math approach to teaching. Annie liked math, which was what caught her attention about the news item, but she missed what the "new" math approach entailed. But she did see all sides in the controversy—the school board, the parents, the kids, and the teachers—all blaming one another for the lower statewide test scores. Everyone sounded lame to Annie. Here they were, all making excuses, all wishing that someone else would do something about the test scores, but nobody thought that they could do anything about it themselves. And as Annie thought about how lame everyone sounded, she became anxious and dizzy, because she realized *she was as lame as those people on the news.* Annie had blamed everyone else, and wished everyone else would fix things—just as she wished that Laura had done more to keep their friendship alive.

But as things became clearer in Annie's mind, she saw that she hadn't done anything except react to what Laura did. Laura had been right. Annie only wrote when Laura first wrote to her, and Annie e-mailed Laura only when Laura first e-mailed her. And, of course, Annie wouldn't

78

have even seen Laura if Laura hadn't invited her out to Midwest U. Annie realized with a sickening sense of guilt that she had never even thought to invite Laura back to her old hometown. Why, Laura might even have wanted to see other friends, and Annie had only thought of herself. No wonder Annie was about to lose her best friend. She hadn't been a friend.

So then, instead of blaming everyone else for her situation, Annie became angry at herself. It was easy, but it also was a relief. Once the anger subsided, she became mysteriously calm—and confident. Confident because she realized that the only way to stay un-angry at herself was to do something about the situation. And she decided she would.

The weird thing was, once she stopped thinking about herself, she could put herself in everyone else's shoes. Captain Cappello, for instance. It was now easy to see why he and Sergeant Hannibal had been skeptical of her story. Not because Laura was making the cuckoo sign, although that hadn't helped. The problem, of course, was that *anyone,* including Dr. D'Orrico, would have a hard time believing that mummies came back to life. *Duh, Annie.* Unless you saw them alive, as Annie—and Laura—had.

And since only she and Laura had seen the mummies alive, they were the only ones who could do anything about them.

Correction, Annie thought. Laura couldn't do anything about it because she was helpless.

And then a remarkable thing happened to Annie. Knowing Laura was helpless made her angry—but only at the mummies. And Annie was the only one who could help Laura.

So she decided she would. Without even feeling sorry for herself. Even though she was scared out of her mind, she knew what she had to do. And she spent the rest of the evening plotting how she would do *something, anything,* to help her best friend. It was suddenly very important for Annie to save Laura, even if it meant that Annie would place herself in danger. That was better than going down without a fight. Much better.

And since she had a plan, she felt confident. Not sure that she would prevail, but confident that she would give it her best shot. Which made her smile.

"So you're nervous, are you?" the witch asked, and Annie shook the cobwebs and said, "Huh?"

"You're nervous. Don't be. It won't hurt. And you'll get your wish. You'll be with your best friend forever. Now come along. *My* oldest best friend can't wait to get a new pair of legs."

Annie gulped and silently followed the witch out of the house, looking like a sheep being led to the slaughter. But only looking that way.

CHAPTER
8

"Come, come along, Annie," the witch sang, sounding exultant, and Annie shuddered. This ugly ancient thing wanted Laura's body—had Laura's body—and its equally repulsive friend wanted Annie's body. Annie pinched herself, feeling her flesh, vowing to keep her mind inside her own head and body.

The witch walked more awkwardly than Laura, so it was strange to see Laura's legs work stiffly as the witch attempted to move quickly in her new body, her arms swinging wildly. The five-thousand-year-old witch was trying to accustom herself to a ten-year-old body. That would work in Annie's favor.

"You've caused us trouble with last night's delay, Annie," the witch said. "Hurry along. Tonight what must be, must happen. We have waited far too long to enter the Next World, and I am anxious to confront that miserable Pharaoh who banished us to the great western desert."

"And what will you do when you see him?" Annie asked.

"Why, we shall exact our revenge," the witch replied.

"Why do you destroy things?" Annie asked. "Why can't you just let things rest in peace?"

The witch stopped and looked up into the air. "Oh, you are a fine one to advise me—you who are lazy and irresponsible in your friendship. That is why you were such an easy mark for us. You react to situations and have no initiative. Laura clued us into that as I took over her body. As our minds began mixing, I read Laura's thoughts. She likes you, of course, but she sees you as a lot of work. But we knew you would come to visit if Laura invited you."

"It was your idea?" Annie asked.

"Of course." The witch laughed. "Laura didn't want you to come here for obvious reasons, but over time we were able to exert our influence through spells."

"Laura didn't want me to come?" Annie said, acting a little hurt.

"Not for the reason you think, you selfish girl. Your friend Laura is smart. She surmised that we needed two bodies, and the college girls didn't fool her. Laura asked you here at our bidding, not hers. She treated you badly when you came for one reason. She wanted you to leave. She was trying to save you."

Of course, Annie thought. That explained Laura's cool behavior over the last weeks and ever since Annie arrived. And it explained Laura's yo-yoing between anger and apologies. She had been fighting the witch inside her. Everything made sense now.

They were getting closer to the Mississippi River, almost near a fork in the path they needed to take to get to the fieldhouse. Annie started inching away from the witch.

"Don't stray, child. I'll not tolerate your defiance any longer." The witch stood and pointed a finger at Annie, but Annie knew enough not to look at the mesmerizing eyes.

Without warning, Annie broke into a sprint when she saw the moving waters of the big river, silvery under the full round moon.

"Come back!" the witch screamed.

Annie yelled over her shoulder, "It's not over, witch!"

Annie sneaked a peek behind her and saw that the witch was hobbling in an ungainly fashion after her. Annie slowed a bit. She wanted the witch to follow her.

"Stop, or we'll make it worse for you, girl. I command you to stop!"

Annie jogged ahead, pumping her arms fast to make the witch think she was sprinting all-out, but Annie conserved energy this way. Besides, the witch couldn't run as fast as Annie. As she ran, she thought about Laura. Laura had tried to save her, even after she realized that she herself couldn't be saved. Annie held back a tear, thinking how brave Laura was, thinking how hard Laura must have been fighting the spells of these witches. Laura's cold behavior had been designed to turn Annie off, to prevent her from coming. And once Annie arrived, Laura had kept at it, getting angry at Annie, trying to make her go back home. Annie wanted to pound her own head against a wall. She knew she couldn't hurt herself because her skull was so thick.

She heard the witch behind her. Annie was a hundred yards from the dock, and she slowed a bit more so the witch would concentrate on her, and not on the river they headed toward. Annie smiled. Her plan, if success-ful, would destroy this witch and get Annie her best friend back.

Annie hopped on top of the gray planks of the dock and her feet slapped hard and loud on wet wood.

As she reached the end of the dock, Annie grabbed a paddle from an open locker and untied the hitch knot tethering a thin canoe to a piling. Annie waited a bit for the witch to reach her, and then, just as the witch bent to grab Annie's shoulder, Annie shoved the paddle against the dock and pushed out into the water. The fiberglass canoe scraped against the pier. The movement caused the witch to fall into the front end of the canoe with a thump. The canoe rocked wildly, but Annie stead-ied the boat using the paddle as a rudder, and soon the witch sat up, grabbing both sides of the canoe to keep herself from falling into the water.

Annie paddled furiously, splashing water all over the place. The only time she had been in a canoe, she had been a passenger, and paddling to keep the canoe straight was harder than she thought. She tried her best, because she needed to get to the middle of the Missis-sippi River for the final part of her plan. She would use the mother of all rivers to defeat the ancient witch, who, as Annie had discovered, could be beaten by water.

"Stop!" the witch hissed. "Turn this boat around. You don't know what you're doing!"

"Oh, yes, I do, witch!" Annie yelled in her face. "I'm saving my best friend, just as she tried to save me. And I'm going to send you back to wherever you're from!"

Annie dug the paddle deep into the water. The canoe wiggled through the black water, and Annie grew more confident with each stroke. Water splashed on the witch, and Annie thought she saw wisps of smoke appear where the water hit skin. She wasn't certain because the air was quite foggy on the river.

The witch began chanting and singing in a high-pitched screech, her head turned toward the shore they had left behind. Annie thought she heard rat squeals in the distance, but it was most likely the wind.

The witch turned, smiling, and tried to make eye contact with Annie, but Annie knew about that trick and kept her gaze averted from the witch's face.

Annie started paddling with the current, finding it easier going. She peered ahead, trying to make out the far shore of the great river, but she saw only the silhouette of trees on the moonlit horizon. She glanced behind her at the shore. It, too, was invisible except for the flat jagged eruptions of trees reaching into the sky.

The witch addressed Annie in a low voice.

"What do you think you're doing?" she asked, her arms rigid on the canoe gunwales. "This has been an unpleasant ride, but you have only delayed things a bit. I told you no more delays." The witch's voice hissed like that of the cobra.

"No more delays, witch," Annie agreed, and she placed the paddle on the bottom of the canoe.

"Pick up the paddle, then," the witch responded, trying to attract Annie's gaze. "Bring us back to shore. Your friend—and my friend—are waiting for us. Let us not be rude."

"Rude, witch?" Annie asked. "How rude have you been? You could care less about anyone or anything except your sorry self. But now I'll show you rude. I want my friend back."

Annie grabbed each side of the canoe, her grip strong. She leaned from side to side, gaining momentum with each pull. The canoe rolled and bobbed, unsteady in the turbulent river current.

"No!" the witch commanded, and this time she held Annie's gaze, but Annie didn't mind, because it would be over in a minute. She thought of last night, when the other witch's legs had dissolved in the pool water.

"It's time for you to disappear, witch. I want Laura back."

Annie heaved the boat back and forth, and the witch tore her gaze away to stare with horror at the water.

"Stop it!" she screamed, her voice shrill and carrying far over the river. "Stop this at once! We must get back tonight!"

"No!" Annie yelled back. "Only one of us has to get back tonight. Me!"

Annie heaved, but the boat wasn't bobbing as much. She pulled and pushed, but the motion was getting steadier. Annie peered over the side as she heard the sound of water bubbling all about, and then she saw that a

86

living sea of gray-brown fur had surrounded the canoe. Rats. Hundreds of them had pressed their small bodies against the canoe hull, applying pressure to oppose of Annie's force, keeping the boat from overturning. Suddenly Annie saw a slithering coil in the water, and then the large olive-brown head of the cobra periscoped out of the river and slid into the witch's lap, where it wrapped its body into a ropelike pile. The cobra brought its head close to Annie and poked its tongue out at her. Annie recoiled, protectively holding the paddle to her body.

Annie glanced at the witch, who was smiling broadly with Laura's smile in Annie's direction.

"Put the wooden paddle gently into the water and bring us back to shore," the witch commanded. Annie locked eyes with the witch, and she dipped the paddle into the water, using it like a rudder to turn back to shore.

"That's a good girl," the witch cooed in her singsong voice. "Soon everything will be done."

Annie paddled hard to fight against the current, tears forming in her eyes as the thundering realization that she had let Laura down hit with agonizing force. She pictured Laura as she had been back east, the smiling, ba-boom–laughing Laura, and she asked for forgiveness. The tears came in a torrent now, and Annie wished someone would come along and take care of things.

Annie, defeated, let her gaze become unfocused, and the power in the witch's gaze did likewise, as if the witch knew Annie realized how powerless she was. Annie's eyes blurred more from the tears and the wind, and she paddled harder, leaving the rats swimming furiously in her wake.

"So you thought you had it in you to defeat me," the witch taunted, and Annie snapped her gaze back, and when their eyes locked, Annie felt the strength in the witch's glare. *No,* she thought, *I can't let Laura down.*

Annie said nothing. Curious, she let her eyes lose focus again while she stared at the witch, and the witch's power diminished once more. Annie relaxed her eyes completely, and the witch suddenly had no hold on her. The cobra's head swayed with the movement of the boat, and Annie glanced at the water and saw only a few rats. She concentrated. It was now or never.

Annie suddenly stood up in the canoe and said, "I didn't *think* I had it, witch. I *knew* I had it. It's water, witch. Water will defeat you."

The witch watched, wide-eyed, as Annie jumped as high as she could and came crashing down in the flimsy stern of the canoe. The bow of the canoe flew up toward the moon, and the witch rocketed in the air as if she had been launched from a fighter jet's ejection seat. The cobra went up with the witch. As the canoe pressed into the water, Annie lost her balance and fell backward into the Mississippi River. The water was cold, but it felt great.

CHAPTER
9

Annie rose to the surface. She gasped for air, but instead sucked in cold brown water as waves from the disturbance caused by the overturned canoe washed over her chin and nose. The water burned her nasal passages. Annie choked, then rose above the waves so she could spit out the water and replace it with air to ease the fire in her lungs.

Treading water, much calmer now with welcome oxygen feeding her muscles, Annie realized she was being swept downstream with the strong river current that had appeared so lazy when she wasn't in it. After a few more breaths Annie rolled onto her back and began swimming a reverse breaststroke so that her head stayed above water. She soon developed a comfortable swimming rhythm, glad that she had worn shorts instead of pants.

The moon chased her through the fog and the dark blue clouds, but its presence reassured Annie.

Annie pointed herself toward the jagged black outline of trees along the shore, taking it easy, smartly angling across the river flow instead of fighting it directly. She sensed that she would hit the muddy riverbank without too much trouble. That was good, because she was getting tired.

Almost relaxed, Annie let out a rebel yell to celebrate her victory over the witch, now probably just a bundle of rags floating in the river. What's more, Laura should be back to herself if the pattern from last night held. Annie had regained her form when the other witch had begun dissolving in the water. She couldn't wait to see Laura now. There was so much to tell her, beginning with a bear hug and words of thanks. Laura had attempted to save Annie, even if her method had been hurtful. Now Annie had been able to pay her back, something that made her proud—and noticeably unselfish. She felt as if a veil had been lifted from her face. No more whining about how circumstances were against Annie. She knew she could change her circumstances with action. You just had to do something, anything, and believe in yourself instead of pitying yourself.

And then Annie's sense of self-satisfaction exploded as abruptly as a popped balloon. The squeaking of hundreds of rats approached her, and the sound suddenly overwhelmed the gurgling water as brown, wet fur rubbed up against her back and legs and arms, even against her face. Annie screamed and wished her legs were covered by pants instead of hanging defenseless from her shorts. The wet rat fur was disgusting.

But the rats didn't attack. They surrounded her, supporting her in the river, as if they wanted to make certain Annie wouldn't drown. Annie was nervous and wondered what this was all about. She had defeated the Rat Witch. Why did these rats seem to be helping her?

Annie felt a rough heavy object slide along her legs and then onto her arm. She watched in horror as the diamond-shaped head slid across her shoulder and came to rest on her neck, the glistening red eyes staring intently. Annie stiffened when she felt the tongue of the giant cobra flicker under her chin, taking her measure, and Annie braced herself for the stinging bite. She squinched her eyes shut and stopped moving, letting herself sink, rigid, unable to move from the fright of sharing her small patch of river water with these beasts whose master she had destroyed. Of course they wanted revenge. But as Annie sank, the rats pressed closer together and she rose up toward the moon again, propelled by the mass of swimming rats.

The cobra's frozen smile broke as the tongue felt Annie's chin again. But it didn't bite. Instead, the cobra slithered across Annie's neck and into the water, swimming away from Annie. The rats parted to make a path for the cobra, and Annie saw its S-shaped body easily propel itself against the current back upriver where the struggle in the canoe had taken place.

Annie gulped in air and tentatively began swimming, and soon most of the rats left her side in groups, but a dozen or so kept her company until her back scraped against a rock. She had made it to shore! Annie felt behind her, afraid she would grab the cobra, but her hand sank into mud, and then the current grabbed her again and she floated away. The rats scampered out of the river and onto the sandy bank, disappearing into shadows cast by a scary-looking leafless tree that blotted out the creamy blue moonlight. The tree branches and roots were thrust into the water, so Annie grabbed at a big root as she glided past the tree. She was surprised at the tug on her shoulders as the river continued along without her. Annie pulled herself to the shore, arm over arm, and soon she could dig her heels into the soft riverbank. She climbed over the small rise and fell on her face, gasping for air, replenishing her muscles, which ached for oxygen.

After a few moments she sat up and pulled her knees to her chin. But she didn't rest long. She had to finish the job, and that meant freeing Laura from the second Rat Witch. Annie stood, her legs cramping, but it felt good to be on solid ground, and she stamped her feet to get the feeling back in them.

Annie estimated she was a half mile or so from the campus. She could see the sidewalk light posts in the distance as she started jogging back to the school. She was determined to get to Laura before the second witch found out about her colleague. Annie glanced around but didn't see any rats. She had a sense that they were scurrying to the gym to squeak about the first witch's tragic—from the witch's perspective—end.

As Annie ran, she heard splashing noises from the river. Was it the cobra? Annie turned and peered at the riverbank. The blue moon lit the river magnificently, and yes, there it was. The cobra was swimming out of the water toward Annie, but it didn't seem to be moving fast. Annie shuddered, thinking how the cobra's tongue had felt under her chin where at one time buttercups held by Laura had reflected colors when they tried to figure out who liked butter. Annie's mouth reacted with distaste as she thought about it.

Annie heard more splashing and assumed the rest of the rat pack was making its way out of the water. But when she glanced back, Annie didn't see a rat. With growing horror, she saw an arm, and then another arm, and then a head surface from the water—Laura's head. But that was impossible. The witch had been destroyed! She *must* have been destroyed! She had been in the water for over fifteen minutes. Annie was certain the witch had dissolved in the limitless waters of the Mississippi. How could this be? Only bandages—not Laura—should be washing ashore.

The body croaked from the river, "Come help, Annie! What am I doing here?"

Annie vaguely heard the voice. She was already a hundred yards closer to the campus—and Laura. Annie didn't understand why the witch hadn't perished in the water, but she didn't have time to think about it, or ask the witch, for that matter. Annie only knew it was essential she get back to the gym. Laura needed her.

"Annie!" the voice from the river screamed. It sounded like the real Laura. But Laura was at the gym with the second witch. Annie was confused. She knew things had gone terribly wrong. All her instincts told her that the body climbing out of the river was that of the witch.

Annie pumped her arms, her mind jumbled. Her well-thought-out plan had gone from victory to disaster, and what was worse, Annie didn't have a clue why. Water defeated these witches. She was certain. She had seen Laura's arm smoke when water hit it, she had seen the witches recoil in horror when she threw water at them, and last night she had certainly seen the other witch's legs dissolve as they lay immersed in the pool water while Annie had miraculously gotten her body back. What had gone wrong tonight?

Could the witch be immune to the effects of the water now that she had fully taken over Laura's body? If that was the case, they were doomed. *Oh, no,* she thought, *I'm a fool.* She thought she had everything figured. And now Laura was trapped in the body of the mummy for all time! Annie lost all the confidence she had built and began to feel sorry for herself again. *Why do all the bad things happen to me?* she thought. *Why?*

Because you are reacting, Annie, a little voice said, and Annie realized it was that part of her that had success-fully planned against the witch, even if the plan had gone awry. *Are you going to give up that easily, Annie?* the voice taunted, and Annie suddenly shouted *"No!"* at the top of her lungs as she ran, feeling the adrenaline rush through her again, but this time it didn't seem yellow with fear, it seemed red hot with determination.

First, Annie thought as she ran, *let me get to Laura. Then we'll deal with the witches.* As she ran, her mind now calm and focused, worked for her. It said, *You*

94

know, Annie Carr, if water won't work on the witch because she has taken over Laura's body, why don't you throw water on the mummy's body that Laura is trapped in?

Of course, Laura thought, *that's it! I'll throw water on the mummy's body which now has Laura trapped, and maybe the process will reverse!* It was the mummy's bandaged body that reacted more violently to the water. It was worth a try.

She smiled, her confidence returning with the new plan. Annie heard scuffling noises behind her and glanced over her shoulder.

Annie yelled and redoubled her running efforts at the sight of the witch, in Laura's body, half skipping, half running, jerking monstrously, but surely gaining on her. The cobra slithered in a blur behind the witch, and rats tumbled over themselves as they hustled on the witch's heels.

"Annie! Why won't you wait!" the witch complained in Laura's voice. "Help me get away from these things!"

Annie saw the gym ahead, and the main double doors were slightly ajar. She squeezed through the doors and slammed them shut in her wake. She looked around and saw a mop stuck in a bucket outside the janitor's closet. Annie grabbed the mop handle and jammed it between the bars that opened the door just as the witch and the rats threw themselves against the glass.

Laura's body screamed, "Open the door!" and attempted to lock her gaze with Annie's, but Annie turned away and rushed down the corridor to the laundry room.

"Annie!" the body screamed. "It's me, Laura! Get me away from these rats!"

Annie stopped, her sneakers squeaking on the polished corridor floor. She yelled back, "Yeah, right!"

"It worked, Annie," Laura's body pleaded. "The water did it. One minute I was in the gym, and the next minute I'm swimming in the river. I'm back, Annie! Hurry. These rats are skeeving me out."

Annie shook her head and water droplets banged against the glass part of the door. The witch—or was it really Laura?—didn't flinch. Laura standing there dripping water made a lot more sense than the witch standing there dripping. No smoke drifted upward. Maybe it *was* Laura, but Annie refused to take any chances.

"Look at me, Annie," the witch—Laura?—said. "Can't you see it's me? I've got my body back. Open the door! Ugh! These rats!"

The girl standing in front of Annie looked just like Laura D'Orrico. Her arms and legs were freckled. Her hair had red highlights. No half dark skin, half freckled skin, which had been the case when Laura had been undergoing her transformation. But if the transformation had taken place, like Annie knew it had, then the witch would look just like this. As a matter of fact, she had looked exactly like Laura tonight right before they left to come to the gym.

The rats formed a semicircle around the girl standing in front of Annie. They looked as if they were about to pounce, but Annie wasn't sure if the rats would pounce on the girl in front of her, or if they were just waiting for the door to open so they could pounce on Annie.

Annie heard hissing, and she turned to look down the hall.

"Chloe!" Annie yelled. "What are you doing here?"

Chloe padded up to the door, arched her back at the rats and Laura on the other side, and hissed again. She peered at Annie and licked her front paws. Then she glanced at Annie once more before heading toward the gym laundry. Chloe disappeared inside the laundry room.

Annie faced the door again. Laura's eyes pleaded with her. If immersing the witch in the Mississippi River had worked and caused the witch to turn back into a mummy, then Laura would have gotten her body back, just as Annie's body had changed back in the pool last night. Oh, it was all so confusing. How could she decide?

"Come on. Let me in and we'll get those witches for good."

That surprised Annie. She said, "If you truly are Laura, you'd want to be a hundred miles from here."

"So I could wait for them to come get me again? No way, Annie. I want to finish this. Now."

Annie squinted. If this was Laura, Annie could really use her company right now. But if it was the witch, Annie didn't want her in the gym. But couldn't the witch find another way in? If Annie let her in, she could keep an eye on her. Well, she certainly wouldn't look her in the eye. It would be all over if the witch mesmerized her.

Annie decided. She lifted the broom handle, but held it like a quarterstaff to keep the rats away when she opened the door. Laura smiled and slid inside and stood in front of the door.

97

"It's about time you got here, Laura," Annie said, smiling, and Laura guffawed, surprising both Annie and Laura, but Annie welcomed it. It was a true Laura laugh.

"Is it really you?" Annie asked, still brandishing the pole.

"Come here," Laura said, and held her arms out for a hug. Annie hugged her friend. She smelled musty from the water.

Annie dropped the pole, staring into Laura's eyes. Why did Laura's eyes seem so dark? Annie heard a buzzing in her ears and smiled at the unbidden thought of her bed at home with new, cool white sheets. As if from above, she saw herself place her head on a pillow, her eyes shut and her legs stretching the length of the bed. She tried to open her eyes, but she knew what had happened. The witch had tricked her.

"Annie! Annie!" Laura said, shaking her. Annie left her dream and found that she was staring at Laura.

"What happened to you, Annie?" Laura said. Her eyes still seemed too dark. But the witch wouldn't have shaken her awake if she had successfully mesmerized her. Would she?

"I must be . . . tired from that . . . ordeal in the river," Annie stammered.

Annie looked at the door. The rats had disappeared.

"Come on," Laura said. "Let's get those witches. It's water that gets them, you said, right?"

"That's right," Annie said, and then she froze. How did Laura know that? She couldn't know that. Annie had mentioned it only once. In the boat. To the witch. Laura didn't know.

Annie kept her horror in check. This wasn't Laura. It was the witch after all, trying to get Annie to come along without a fight. With that realization, the fight began to leave Annie. It didn't matter anyway. Water hadn't worked. Her plan hadn't worked. Her friendship hadn't worked. Annie decided to play along with the witch. Maybe she could think of something to get her best friend out of this mess, but she was just plain worn out, physically and mentally. No more head games. No more running.

"Okay, witch, you win," Annie said.

The witch turned and smiled. "What a smart girl."

"Because I figured out you were the witch?"

"No, Annie. Because you realize how hopeless your situation is and you'll behave now. Remember, you'll be with your best friend forever. That's what you wished for, right?"

Annie shrugged. "I guess you're right."

"No more guessing, Annie. You put up a brave resistance, and my sister witch is fortunate to get such a courageous body. We'll use your bodies well in the Next World. Come now. Let us finish it."

Annie fumed at the witch's arrogance. Things were hopeless, but if this witch thought that Annie would go meekly to the slaughter, she was wrong. The witch's arrogance made Annie vow to fight to the last, no matter how helpless things appeared.

The witch led Annie to the laundry room. Inside, Annie saw two mummies, one of whom was Laura. The second mummy had no legs and was face to face with Chloe, whose back was arched.

The witch in Laura's body said, "What are you doing here?"

The second witch scampered on her knuckles toward them.

"That cat! She appeared from nowhere and created havoc in the subterranean room, scattering candles all about. I feared fire. So I brought the girl and the potion up here. We're ready!"

Annie looked at the real Laura, grotesquely encased in the mummy's body. She held a beaker of blue potion in her bandaged hands. Her eyes stared unseeing, zombie-like. Her face was skeletal and disgusting, and Annie glared, horrified, knowing she would soon look like that.

"Drink, Laura," the witch who had stolen Laura's body said. Annie watched as her best friend, or what was left of her, raised the beaker to her lips.

CHAPTER
10

"Wait!" Annie screamed.

The witches turned their heads to Annie.

"I thought the transformation had been completed. That's why I thought the water didn't dissolve you!" Annie stated. The thought gave Annie energy. She needed it to concentrate.

The witch guffawed in Laura's voice. "Oh, child, you are not that smart after all." She turned and stared at the beaker of blue liquid. "Drink," she commanded.

"Wait!" Annie begged. She needed time. Something was beginning to click in her mind about the water. The answer was there, but the crucial detail eluded her. Things were happening much too fast. She needed time to think. She was still so tired, but she needed to hang on. "Take my body!" she wailed.

The witch shook her head. "But of course we will. Have you forgotten my spiritual sister?"

The legless witch hobbled on her stumps toward Annie. Her horrible mummy face split as her lips parted, revealing greenish yellow teeth and blackened gums. Dirty bandages swirled and trailed along the floor as the witch swung about on her knuckles. Fetid air invaded Annie's nostrils as the legless witch spoke.

"I need your body. Especially those legs. And you shall be welcome to this half body which you created, miserable child."

Annie grimaced as an image of herself trapped inside the monstrous bundle of rags facing her propped up on its knuckles played across her mind's eye. If she drank the blue potion, she would spend eternity trapped inside the petrified body. She told herself there was no way that she would let the potion get near her. But what to do? Fight or flight? She felt the adrenaline rush through her bloodstream. This time it was orange, a combination of yellow fear and red rage.

As Annie looked around the room for an escape, she noticed that the door frame was filled by the swaying cobra. Rats hovered in all corners. Fleeing was impossible. Flight or . . . fight. Annie steeled herself. She had only one option.

"Drink!" the head witch commanded once more.

Annie watched the second witch pirouette to see Laura—what was left of her—finish the potion. Rags from the witch's stumps trailed across Annie's sneakers. Annie bent over and grabbed a fistful of bandages.

"No, Laura!" Annie screamed, and she yanked the bandages with all her strength.

The legless witch flopped onto her back as Annie spun around and pulled hard, swinging the witch along the smooth linoleum floor of the laundry. The witch moaned as Annie spun her, and her long fingernails made a piercing noise as she frantically grabbed at the floor to stop the spinning. The bandages started unwinding from the centrifugal force competing between Annie and the witch, so Annie grabbed fistfuls of rags and piled them at her feet while she kept spinning the witch.

Rats attempted to grab hold of the witch, but her body sent them scattering as it whirled faster and faster. The witch was now rolling and spinning at the same time, and more and more of her leathery black body was exposed as the bandages were pulled away.

Annie noticed something long and curved moving side to side toward her. The cobra was speeding directly at Annie, but it suddenly pulled upright. Annie heard a loud yowl. Chloe! Chloe jumped in front of the snake and swung her paws at the cobra's head in a blur, and she connected, knocking the cobra aside. Chloe grew menacingly tall as she arched her back, keeping the cobra from attacking Annie.

The head witch in Laura's body scowled and walked jerkily to the spinning mass of Annie, rags, and legless mummy. Annie gave a tremendous tug and the bandages snapped. The legless witch vaulted away from Annie and crashed right into the head witch, whose mouth hung open in shock. The two witches careened backward and thudded into the door of one of the industrial washing

103

machines, the collision forcing the front-loading door to pop open.

"Get off!" the witch screamed, pushing her legless companion, who rolled along the floor, dazed and completely off balance from her unwanted merry-go-round ride. The witch inhabiting Laura's body stood, holding Laura's head with Laura's hands, and Annie rushed forward, but Chloe beat Annie to the washing machine.

Chloe jumped right at the witch, and Annie watched as Laura's body tumbled into the large washing machine to get away from the cat. Annie yelled, "Good girl, Chloe!" as she slammed the washing machine door shut. Without taking the time to think, Annie pulled change from her pocket. She yanked her hand out too quickly, and coins went rolling along the floor.

Chloe pounced on two quarters, one to each front paw, and Annie scrambled on all fours to retrieve the rest of the money. She fumbled as she placed the quarters in the change slot.

The witch in the machine banged hard on the glass door, and her muffled screams unnerved Annie, but she concentrated, got the quarters aligned, and jammed the silver handle home, starting the machine. Annie set it at permanent press and made the water hot.

She stepped back. Water filled the machine as the tumbler spun, and Annie saw with relief that small tendrils of smoke rose from the witch's—Laura's—skin. Laura! The witch in the machine was staring past Annie's shoulder as she spun. The witch's eyes were dark, intense, focused, attempting to mesmerize . . . someone. Who?

Annie spun around and saw that Laura—in the mummy's body—was staring at the witch in the machine, and Annie screamed when she saw that the beaker of blue potion was touching her friend's lips.

"No, Laura!" Annie screamed again and ran, diving at her best friend. She grabbed the blue beaker and set it down on a bench. She shook Laura, hard, but Laura just stared like a zombie back at the witch. Annie turned and saw the witch, still smoking lightly, tumbling in the machine.

Annie wondered how the witch was surviving the water of the washing machine, and she was awed thinking about the fifteen minutes the witch had survived in the Mississippi River. What was she missing? Water affected these mummies. She had seen it. First, when Laura had stuck her hand in the washing machine the first day Annie had arrived on campus. Then again when Annie had thrown water at the witches in the subterranean room, and most spectacularly when the second witch had chased Annie into the swimming pool and lost her legs. But the witch hadn't smoked at all in the Mississippi. Why? And why would the witch billow smoke in the swimming pool and barely smoke at all when Annie threw water at the both of them? Why, even Laura's arm had smoked far more when she was washing that load of white clothes—and then the answer hit Annie full force.

Annie ran to the shelf where lost socks and laundry baskets shared space with all sorts of laundry bleach. Annie grabbed a white bottle and ran over to the washing machine. She lifted the lid covering the bleach loading slot, opened the bottle, and splashed half the contents down the chute.

Annie stepped back and looked into the round window. The witch began screaming, and then white smoke exploded inside the machine, expanding like a fizzing tablet dropped into water, and then the smoke obscured everything inside the machine except the wails of the mummy witch. Smoke billowed out of the machine, and then a blue liquid mixture seeped out of every seam in the white washing machine. The door exploded open, and suds and lily white bandages shot out and draped over the door opening.

Annie turned and saw Laura—the real Laura—standing where Annie had left her. But now, instead of being trapped inside the mummy witch's body, she wore her own skin and bones. Laura looked around in confusion, shaking her head. She locked gazes with Annie.

"Annie?" she asked. "Annie?"

Annie walked toward Laura. "Yes, Laura. It's me. We won. We *won!*"

"Annie?" Laura asked again, shaking her head, focusing her eyes.

"What?" Annie asked, smiling. She felt vast relief.

"Annie! Look out!" Laura shouted, pointing past Annie.

Annie froze. Then she spun about.

As she did, she felt her legs go out from under her as she tripped over something. Falling, she saw a mass of bandages trailing from the second mummy, scampering on one hand's knuckles while she lifted Annie's leg with her other hand. Annie hit her head on the floor and lights exploded across the inside of her forehead. She tried to rise, but the witch had scrambled onto her chest, pinning her down. The witch reached to the side and picked up the beaker of blue liquid.

As Annie started to scream *"No!"* the witch poured the liquid into Annie's open mouth. The blue liquid felt ice cold and molten hot as it raced down Annie's throat.

"I told you I wanted your legs!" the witch shouted. The witch pulled herself back and leaned on her arms facing Annie.

Annie sat up, but that was all she could do. Her toes tingled and went numb. Pins and needles pricked her feet, the sole of her heel itched, and then her ankles tingled while her feet went numb. That process inched its way up her legs—pins and needles attacked, unbearable itching replaced the tingling, and Novocain-like numbness completed the cycle.

When the feeling reached Annie's calf, she looked down and saw that *her feet were gone.*

Next her legs began disappearing, and Annie moaned. She looked across and saw the witch smiling, her eyes closed, and then Annie glanced along the witch's body. The witch was growing legs—Annie's legs.

Now the numbness reached Annie's chest, and she saw that her lower torso was now that of the legless witch—leathery, paper-thin, covered with dirty rags.

Annie saw that the witch would soon completely possess her body. Her face was beginning to take shape over the grotesque mask of the mummy. It would all be over soon.

Annie began crying. She wouldn't be best friends with

Laura anymore, not as humans—or as mummies. Only Annie would be a mummy. But despite her hopelessness, Annie felt good about one thing. She had hung in there when things seemed impossible, and she had saved her best friend by defeating the first arrogant mummy witch. She decided to concentrate on that thought as she changed into a mummy. She had conquered her selfishness and her helplessness, and it had been for good. And in a strange way, that knowledge helped her accept her own fate.

Annie, groggy now, looked over to see her best friend one more time, but Laura was gone. She must have left to get help, even if it was too late. But that was okay, because for weeks and days Laura had very bravely tried to save Annie by sacrificing their friendship. And it was the only thing that Laura could have done, because Laura hadn't been able to trust Annie at that point because Annie hadn't known how to get past her own feelings. Even though it was too late, Annie hoped Laura trusted her now.

Annie felt something grip her head, and she braced herself for the tingling, the itching, and the numbness which would seal her fate forever. Instead, she heard a voice. Her best friend's voice.

"Annie! Annie! Wake up! Now!"

Annie looked at her friend. Laura wore a frown. Annie just wanted to sleep.

"Annie! Tell me how!" Annie followed Laura's gaze. The witch was still transforming, and like Annie was incapable of moving while their bodies switched. *What was*

108

Laura saying? Annie asked herself. She was too groggy to concentrate.

"Annie Carr, wake up or I'll give you a noogie! I will!"

"Huh?" Annie asked. *A noogie?*

"What did you do to the first witch?"

Annie closed her eyes. She was jolted awake by a burning sensation in her scalp. "Cut it out!" she yelled.

"No!" Laura said, rubbing her knuckles into Annie's hair harder.

"Ow!" Annie said, and suddenly things became clear. Laura was trying to keep her awake. And asking her something. Something about . . .

"The white bottle!" Annie yelled.

Laura dropped Annie's head. "Where?" she shouted.

Annie pointed toward the washing machine with her head, because her arms wouldn't respond. The tingling attacked Annie's neck and chin, and quickly spread to her lips. The itching and numbness followed. Annie's eyes started to itch terribly, and then everything went black.

Unable to see, Annie began dreaming. In her dream she saw Laura standing over the witch, tilting the bottle, liquid splashing everywhere, and then Annie felt pinpoints burning her forehead, followed by itching, but this time instead of numbness, the itching and burning intensified.

Annie's vision came into focus, and then her hearing came back. The witch was screaming. Annie's eyes focused and she saw white smoke billowing like a mad magician's act, and then she saw Laura through the haze, standing over the witch, the last of the liquid dripping from the bottle.

Annie looked down. Her legs were coming back. And where the witch had been, only rags were left.

Laura bent down and hugged Annie hard, not letting her go. The girls stayed that way for a long time, hugging and rocking, not speaking, both crying.

Laura finally helped Annie to stand.

Annie looked about. The only sign of the mummies was the rags scattered on the floor and hanging from the washing machine. The beaker of potion, now empty, lay on its side next to the bundle of rags. There were no rats and there was no cobra. In a corner Chloe licked her paws as if nothing had happened.

Laura grabbed Annie's hand.

"How did you figure it out?" Laura asked.

"The bleach?" Annie replied.

Laura nodded. "Bleach?"

Annie smiled, weary beyond belief. She just wanted to find a bed.

"At first I thought water would defeat them. There was a pattern. That time you stuck your hand in the wet clothes, how your skin smoked when water touched it. The witches were afraid of water, too. The witch lost her legs in the pool, and the transformation process reversed itself. But then the Mississippi River—I'll tell you about it later—didn't destroy the witch."

"So how did you make a connection to bleach?"

"Not bleach. Chlorine. Trace amounts of chlorine in tap water, so little smoke. Lots of chlorine in the pool, so big smoke. Lots of smoke when you stuck your hand in the wet clothes you were washing—white clothes, and you used chlorine bleach. Easy, finally. When I poured the chlorine bleach in the washing machine—poof! No more witch."

"Poof?" Laura asked.

"Poof, poof," Annie replied, looking from the washing machine to the rags at their feet. "Poof, poof, whiter than white."

Laura guffawed an Olympian laugh. Then it trailed away.

"What will we tell my father?"

CHAPTER
11

A few days later Annie said good-bye to Laura and Dr. D'Orrico at the bus station where everything had begun.

"I'm real sorry about your mummies, Dr. D'Orrico. But thanks so much for having me."

Dr. D'Orrico smiled and shrugged.

"These things happen, Annie," he replied. "Never to me before, but I'll deal with it. Mummies and artifacts are valuable. People have stolen mummies before, mainly to sell to private collectors who can't seem to get enough of the past. But thieves usually don't leave the bandages behind. I don't get it. The only thing missing besides the bodies is one of those replica scarab rings which we placed on the mummy. The real ring—and other jewelry—is still at the bank. So the thieves got the mummies and a fake ring."

"You're taking it well, Dad," Laura said, her arm draped around her dad's arm.

Dr. D'Orrico smiled again. "Well, it helps that you're not acting like a stranger anymore. Annie, I think you had a positive effect on my little girl. She and Chloe are even buddies again. Come back anytime. Open invitation."

Annie beamed back. "Well, I just might take you up on that." *Because,* she thought, *if I want to stay best friends with Laura, I can't wait around for her to call and write, feeling sorry for myself. This trip gave me the confidence to see how important it is to take matters into my own hands. Especially when it comes to friendship.* "This trip had a positive effect on me, too, Dr. D'Orrico. Thank you both for the kitten." Annie stroked the downy soft fur which stood straight up from the little gray kitten's bony head.

"Your bus driver is waving to you, Annie," Dr. D'Orrico said, pointing up the bus stairs.

Annie and Laura hugged. Laura whispered, "Thanks, Annie. See you real soon." She gave Annie a hearty slap on the back and fiddled with her backpack. Annie pulled away as Laura threatened her with a noogie, hitching her backpack onto her shoulder and squeezing past Laura to get to the bus door. She caught a whiff of something musty—like wet newspapers that had dried. She shook her head and climbed on the bus.

What was that smell?

It couldn't have been Laura. Laura's skin—and Annie's—had completely healed.

Annie took a seat at the back of the bus, vaguely uneasy. She looked around. The scent was stronger.

Annie placed her backpack on her lap and let the kitten use it as a bed. But the kitten couldn't get comfortable, and suddenly it arched its back and pawed at the backpack.

Annie moved the kitten away and felt a bulge in a zipper pocket. She unzipped the pocket, and the musty smell invaded her nostrils. She reached in and pulled out a soft package. Dirty linen bandages. Not bright white linen bandages.

Annie and the kitten competed to open the bandages, the kitten sinking its tiny claws into the thin cloth.

Annie unwrapped the package and gasped.

The scarab ring Laura had worn as she was transformed rested on a note.

Annie opened the note and read two words: ". . . friends forever . . ."

Annie sniffed the linen wrapper and smiled. Musty. Laura hadn't been musty after all. *Just the linen, right?* Annie's smile turned slightly crooked.

As the bus pulled out of the station with a roar, Annie heard the loud guffaw of Laura D'Orrico. She'd have to call Laura as soon as she got home.

Epilogue: The Midnight Society

Annie called Laura and wrote to Laura and e-mailed Laura first for quite a while, but soon the girls settled into one of those rare give-and-take friendships that made both of them cherish the time they spent together.

Of course, no one ever saw those mummies again, although Annie and Laura did get to see many ancient bandaged bodies when Dr. D'Orrico took the girls with him on a field trip to Egypt.

And whenever Annie felt sorry for herself or her situation, she stepped back and asked herself what was really going on, and before too long, she came up with an answer that usually had her fixing things by herself. And she liked the control she gained over her life.

So that's my story. Look, Frank, we used four logs tonight—oh, I forgot one thing. That dirty old bandage that Laura had used to wrap the ring? Annie left it on the bus by accident. And a kid picked it up when she was on her way to New York City to visit her best friend, wondering why it had a blue stain, and by the time she got to the Big Apple, she couldn't understand why her skin had gotten darker. So she threw the bandage out in a garbage can and the wind took it and sent it flying high up in the air, and she didn't see where it landed. . . .

But don't you worry. It probably didn't land anywhere near you . . . or your best friend.

Until next time, pleasant dreams. Put out the fire, Frank. I declare this meeting of the Midnight Society closed.

ABOUT THE AUTHOR

Mark Mitchell lives in Connecticut with his wife, Marie, and their children, Allie, Claire, and Ted, and a dog named Mikey. He used to work for banks in New York City and Connecticut. Now he writes books and travels with his family.

My favorite part of summer is

- ❏ anytime I'm not in the car.
- ❏ burying my dad in the sand while he's taking a nap.
- ❏ asking my mom "Are we having fun yet?" every five minutes and then telling her I was just reading the title of this cool activity book out loud.

Are We Having Fun Yet?

Summer Activities Inspired By

NICKELODEON MAGAZINE

 A MINSTREL® BOOK

Published by Pocket Books

Read Books. Earn Points. Get Stuff!

NICKELODEON® and
MINSTREL® BOOKS

Now, when you buy any book with the special Minstrel® Books/Nickelodeon "Read Books, Earn Points, Get Stuff!" offer, you will earn points redeemable toward great stuff from Nickelodeon!

Each book includes a coupon in the back that's worth points. Simply complete the necessary number of coupons for the merchandise you want and mail them in. It's that easy!

Nickelodeon Magazine.	4 points
Twisted Erasers	4 points
Pea Brainer Pencil	6 points
SlimeWriter Ball Point Pen	8 points
Zzand	10 points
Nick Embroidered Dog Hat	30 points
Nickelodeon T-shirt	30 points
Nick Splat Memo Board	40 points

- Each book is worth points (see individual book for point value)
- Minimum **40** points to redeem for merchandise
- Choose anything from the list above to total at least **40** points. Collect as many points as you like, get as much stuff as you like.

What? You want more?!?!
Then Start Over!!!

NICKELODEON/MINSTREL BOOKS POINTS PROGRAM

Official Rules

1. *HOW TO COLLECT POINTS*

Points may be collected by purchasing any book with the special Minstrel®/Nickelodeon "Read Books, Earn Points, Get Stuff!" offer. Only books that bear the burst "Read Books, Earn Points, Get Stuff!" are eligible for the program. Points can be redeemed for merchandise by completing the coupons (found in the back of the books) and mailing with a check or money order in the exact amount to cover postage and handling to Minstrel Books/Nickelodeon Points Program, P.O. Box 7777-G140, Mt. Prospect, IL 60056-7777. Each coupon is worth points. (See individual book for point value.) Copies of coupons are not valid. Simon & Schuster is not responsible for lost, late, illegible, incomplete, stolen, postage-due, or misdirected mail.

2. *40 POINT MINIMUM*

Each redemption request must contain a minimum of 40 points in order to redeem for merchandise.

3. *ELIGIBILITY*

Open to legal residents of the United States (excluding Puerto Rico) and Canada (excluding Quebec) only. Void where taxed, licensed, restricted, or prohibited by law. Redemption requests from groups, clubs, or organizations will not be honored.

4. *DELIVERY*

Allow 6-8 weeks for delivery of merchandise.

5. *MERCHANDISE*

All merchandise is subject to availability and may be replaced with an item of merchandise of equal or greater value at the sole discretion of Simon & Schuster.

6. *ORDER DEADLINE*

All redemption requests must be received by January 31, 1999, or while supplies last. Offer may not be combined with any other promotional offer from Simon & Schuster. Employees and the immediate family members of such employees of Simon & Schuster, its parent company, subsidiaries, divisions and related companies and their respective agencies and agents are ineligible to participate.

COMPLETE THE COUPON AND MAIL TO
NICKELODEON/MINSTREL POINTS PROGRAM
P.O. BOX 7777-G140
MT. PROSPECT, IL 60056-7777

NICKELODEON

MINSTREL® BOOKS

NAME_____

ADDRESS_____

CITY _____ STATE _____ ZIP _____

THIS COUPON WORTH FIVE POINTS
Offer expires January 31, 1999

I have enclosed _____coupons and a check/money order (in U.S. currency only) made payable to "Nickelodeon/Minstrel Books Points Program" to cover postage and handling.

❏ 40–75 points (+ $3.50 postage and handling)
❏ 80 points or more (+ $5.50 postage and handling)

1464-01(2of2)